Borderline

ABE DANCER

A Black Horse Western

ROBERT HALE · LONDON

© Abe Dancer 2003
First published in Great Britain 2003

ISBN 0 7090 7292 9

Robert Hale Limited
Clerkenwell House
Clerkenwell Green
London EC1R 0HT

Typeset by
Derek Doyle & Associates, Liverpool.
Printed and bound in Great Britain by
Antony Rowe Limited, Wiltshire

Borderline

Will Mitten, the US Marshal of Newburg, has to transport Franklin Poole across New Mexico to stand trial for murder. But Poole used to be a friend, someone with whom the marshal shared a dramatic childhood. And, to complicate matters, there is some doubt as to whether Poole is guilty. But when Poole and his treacherous cohorts break free from their captive chains, the real dilemma for Will begins.

On a terrifying stage-coach run from the deserted mining town of Blushing Lode to Arroyo Hondo and the Colorado border, Will Mitten finds himself not only at the mercy of his erstwhile prisoners and a band of murderous renegades, but also the target of a lawless and revengeful posse.

Can Will survive it all?

1

Out Of The Ashes

It was the tail end of August, and Captain Bewle Callister was getting anxious. From Wyoming, he'd entered Utah Territory with high expectations. The States of Illinois and Missouri were far to the east, but their combined stance against the Mormon fraternity could still help the promotion campaign of a ruthless officer in the federal army.

In the stifling heat of his tent, the captain sat and listened to Valentine Quirrel. The man was a scout who'd heard of a wagon train moving north from Salt Lake City. They comprised families of salvationists, en route to Ogden and Brigham City. But the party were stubborn, and long-suffering of danger, thought they didn't have need of a self-protectionist guerilla group calling themselves the Mormon Raiders.

'Gimme a few more days,' Quirrel told Callister. 'I can almost smell that hot bread an' sweet apple pie.'

Callister sat frustrated and impatient, less than a mile beneath the timberline of the Uinta Mountains. 'I'd be surprised if you could smell anythin' through that whiskey haze o' yours. You've got one week,' he rasped.

After Quirrel had left, Callister took his telescope and stood in the fresh air for a while. He vainly searched for a wisp of smoke, rise of larks, anything that might give a lead to the whereabouts of the Mormon encampment.

It was three days later that Quirrel reported back. He'd backtracked the train to a camp along Bitter Creek. One hundred and fifty miles out of Fort Rawlins, Captain Callister issued instructions to his troops. He made a decision to attack the following dawn.

Because of the pitch blackness, and closeness of the tree stands along the banks of the creek, Quirrel had difficulty in locating the sign of hoof and wheel marks. It wasn't dawn as planned, but mid-morning before the men moved forward.

Callister divided his company into two columns. The first would attack from the north, head-on, with orders to fire at will. The second column would ford the creek to scatter the small remuda. But they would also draw their sabres.

The Mormon party were few in number. For the last few miles of their journey they'd travelled untroubled and had mistakenly turned back their scouts and protective guns. They were mostly old men and women with their grandchildren. They could only

6

flee in terror, under the sweeping blades and indis-
criminate gunfire of the attack. Skirmishers shot at
livestock, lay bare the meagre, basic supplies of cloth-
ing and food. Quirrel looked for relics and religious
trinkets, sought mythical gold plates. They would sell
them on, historical trophies of the Mormon crushing.
Captain Callister sat blood-crazed, as his horse skittered and tripped among the whimpers of the dying.
The Mormons were defenceless, and within minutes
the only sounds to be heard were those of frightened
dogs, horses and a few mules. The only signs of movement were ashen tendrils rising from trampled break-
fast fires and burned wagons.

But the soldiers hadn't quite cleared all sign of life.
There were two youngsters whose breathing caught
the attention of a semi-loup. The dog circled from a
safe distance, then nudged inquisitively with its wet,
splattered nose. The two children were huddled in a
shawl, both trembling under the low swirling smoke.

Under new government orders the Company returned
to swill out any lasting remains of their engagement.
But they were nervous, and waited five days for the
Mormon Raiders to appear from Salt Lake or Brigham
City. When it didn't happen they quickly finished off
their grisly work. With rakes and shovels they scoured
the earth; made bare runnels across shallow graves
where the devout brethren had once been camped.

Among the Company, there were two civilians. One
was employed by Washington to act as a land negotia-
tor, and the other as a post trader. During the mass

7

burial, the trader, Rimmer Poole, in his desire for secreted doodads or finely made tools, lashed out with his boot at the attentions of a scavenger dog. He'd seen a handmade blanket. He tugged at the bulky material, and was astonished when he uncovered two small bodies lying in the cold grey ash. They were boys, about three years old. But no more than a year separated them, and they clawed silently at the ground in mute fear.

Poole was instinctively on his guard, and he cautiously dragged the bodies towards some grass closer to the creek. He looked around him for any sign of being observed, and then dispatched the children into a shallow at the base of the clump. He feigned an official-looking task, and returned to his horse to stuff the blanket into a pouch. He poured a handful of barley pellets into a raggedy army cap, and casually tossed it in the direction of the unknowing children. He would mention it to a woman acquaintance when they pulled into Rock Springs in two or three days time. That was the town that provided rest and recuperation for the Company – where the troopers would picket and re-provision, before circling east back to Rawlins.

Peggy Mitten clucked her buckskin forward. She edged it nearer the clearing that was almost fifty miles from Rock Springs. The spot was more or less how it had been described by Rimmer Poole, only now it was crawling with pariah dogs, sniffing and scratching across the barren ground. They were hideously thin with mange, the fur eaten away to raw skin. They were fearful and depraved and it made Peggy's skin crawl.

There was a cloying, fruity cut to the air, and Peggy retched at the wisps of putrid gas that were already seeping through the earth. The horse baulked, and as she turned its head away from the dogs, Peggy caught sight of the vultures sweeping slowly in great circles less than a hundred feet above them. She spat contemptuously, looked towards the creek through the clusters of grass. She found what she was looking for and nudged the horse slowly across the soft, dipping ground. The grubby, half-starved children were kneeling in the shallow water, playing with the silver ripples as they weaved between the folds of their crumpled breeches.

From what Poole told her, the children had probably gone without food for at least five days. Since then, there had been another shelterless bout of survival on nothing but cress, water, and a handful of army horse-pellets. Her smile was genuine, but her sarcastic thoughts were for Rimmer Poole. In Peggy, the trader had sensed a basic emptiness, but what she saw in front of her would hardly make her life in Rock Falls full or complete.

Peggy cautiously climbed from the buckskin and stooped to pick up a crumpled, blue army cap. She reckoned it was the ninth or tenth day, and was already considering Tenner as a first name for one of the boys. She'd slip in Will, to make a convincing tag, though. Yep, not bad she thought, Tenner Will Mitten. She'd do her bit, her best, for one of them, but Poole could help out for the other one.

2

Beyond The Border

It was nearly eight hundred miles south-east of Rock Falls where the "blue whistler" brought ill fortune to northern New Mexico. It ran through the grassland, pressed out any sign of new-shooting grass. It was early spring, but it dried the ground and shrunk the water-courses, whipped back the clouds that might have provided rain. The wind blew rough dust into the near forty head of Callister scatterlings that Franklin Poole had brought down from the high pasture along the Sangre de Cristos. He wanted to turn the stock into the home pasture while there was still some graze.

It was first dark when he shouldered the cattle through the gate of the pasture. Yellow pin pricks of light from the town of Eagle Spring were beginning to shine across the Horse Creek.

As he approached the low-built ranch house, rode into the yard, he realized the place was deserted. The house and outbuildings were in darkness. Nothing moved; the whole place was too quiet and still for anybody to be living there. The hay and feedstocks were gone and fences were down. The pasture was as bare and hard-packed as a barn floor, and stretched right into the valley.

The outlook was that bleak, but his horse pricked its ears and Poole wondered. It turned its rump to the wind, snorted with interest, disquiet.

'Is that you, Deadmeat?' someone called, cautiously questioned.

Frank thought he recognized the voice that came from the ramshackle barn off to his left.

'Yeah,' he said, stifled and gruff to disguise his voice. He dismounted vigilantly and let the reins drop, made his way to the door that was hanging off its hinges. He peered into the dark interior and saw shadowy movement, heard the unmistakable noise of pushing horses, the snuffle of unrest.

He stepped in, and was immediately confronted by the heavy, feral odour of wild animal. Louis Callister stepped out of the darkness, holding a fancy single-action Colt.

'Where . . . where's Deadmeat?' Callister stammered with ill-concealed worry and surprise. 'What the hell you doin' here, Poole?'

'I came lookin' for home pasture . . . got me some o' your pa's goddamn cattle. Never reckoned on findin' a Callister stealin' his own remuda. That's what you're doin' aint it Louis? Sellin' on your old man's saddle brokes. That sure takes some special kind o' family feelin'.'

In the low dusty light, Poole saw Callister's eyes blaze with the anger of being caught red-handed. It was scary, and he backed off a step. He felt his boot heel move the shank of a hay fork and he stopped. He edged fractionally to the side and twisted back his right hand.

'What you goin' to do, Louis?' he asked as calm as he could.

'I aint goin' to do anythin'. I'll leave that to Deadmeat. He'll be here soon. Deadmeat's half-bear . . . don't leave anythin' alive. Unless it's horses or mules or women he skins 'em.'

'He's goin' to kill me then?' Poole asked explicitly.

'Not straight off. He'll chew on your liver while you're still alive . . . you won't go to waste. I'll bury what's left. Why you so interested?'

'I just wanted to make sure I'm doin' the right thing,' he said. With that, Poole grasped the shaft of the fork and in one smooth, fast movement he swung it up. He thrust it away from him, hard and low into Callister's belly.

'You're scum, Louis. I'm just sorry your pa aint ever goin' to know it,' he said, shaking with foreboding over the corner he'd got himself into.

Callister gasped and snatched at the trigger of his Colt. The gun exploded, but the bullet went up and through the roof of the barn. Poole levered up Callister's body on the fork, watched while the man's contorted fingers dragged at the rusting tines. Poole then gave a mighty heave, and slammed the body back and down onto the floor of a dirt-covered stall.

The horses were stamping now, squealing with fear. Poole kicked down the barn doors. '*Vamoose*,' he yelled wondering how close the man called Deadmeat and his men were. He knew they'd take the horses, and the forty head of prime young beeves.

Will found Poole's horse tethered in one of the outbuildings. He turned it loose, after taking the canteen of water and a rolled-up Navajo rug.

Louis Callister was Bewle Callister's only child. In years to come he'd be the inheritor of Callister land and its many holdings. But with his death, his distraught, enraged father would organize the whole of Horse Creek to bring the killer to heel. Within hours, there'd be a brutish posse snapping at Poole's trail, all contending for the significant prize that Canister would be offering.

With nothing more than that on his mind. Franklin Poole walked to his horse. He looked to the Sangre de Cristos, the borders of Colorado and beyond to Utah.

3

Return To Eagle Spring

Three men walked their horses across the mud-ruts, up to the steps of the low, sun-baked building. There was a painted sign that spelled out, 'The River Bend Saloon,' hanging above the single swing door. Franklin Poole looked intently at the Chinaman, then nodded at another man, Charlie Chumser. He held up the palm of his hand. 'Stay with the horses, Charlie. I won't be needin' you.'

Inside, the rich aromas of frontiersmen, tobacco and beer embraced Poole and the Chinaman. There were a few tables, a few customers. Like everything in that corner of New Mexico, everything appeared to be bleached, shrouded in a thin film of pale sand.

Poole walked slowly to the bar. 'Two whiskeys.' he told the barman. For a few moments he looked into the mirror behind the counter, made contact with the reflections of two men sitting behind him.

One of them was Chester Quirrel, over from Newburg to see Jabber Nibbs. There was a near empty bottle on their table and two glasses. Quirrel looked at the reflection of Poole for some moments before he spoke to Nibbs.

'I know that feller from somewhere,' he said. 'You have a look Jabe . . . recognize either of 'em?'

Nibbs turned, had a thoughtful look at both men. 'No,' he said. 'I don't think they're wanted here.'

Poole looked back to the barman. 'You know anythin' of an ol' feller named Poole – Rimmer Poole?' he asked him. 'Used to freight hardware up from Newburg. Liked a drink, an' weren't too fussy where he got it. He'd more'n likely have come in here.'

'I'm new in town,' the barman replied. 'Don't know spit from biscuit.'

'You'll go far then,' Poole said dourly.

The Chinaman nodded once sharply and grinned as he took his whiskey.

From the table, Quirrel pushed back his chair. 'Jeez that's it,' he said. 'It's him. *Frank Poole*. It was years back, but I reckon he's still wanted for killin' Louis Callister.'

Poole sensed something had happened. His cool stare remained, but his stance hardened.

Quirrel unwound himself from the table. He got to his feet, stepped unsteadily forward. Poole turned to face the disturbance. He spoke with a thin smile across his face. 'Somethin' bitin' your backside, mister?'

15

Quirrel swayed closer, but Nibbs was suddenly behind him, holding him back. 'This is sheriff's business, Chester, not yours,' he said, loud enough to implicate himself.

Quirrel shook away Nibbs's restraining arm. 'That gun you're wearin', Poole? Is it the one you used to murder Louis Callister?' he demanded.

The Chinaman's black eyes darted around the bar. He made a light hissing sound, stuck a hand inside the top pocket of his bib overalls.

Poole didn't take his eyes from Quirrel. 'You wouldn't want to go mistakin' me for a murderer, mister. Only a fool'd do that. I came into town peaceable, an' that's how I aim to go.'

Quirrel's eyes narrowed and he made a clumsy move for his gun. Poole swore, took one pace forward and drove his fist up into Quirrel's jaw. As Quirrel crumpled, he managed to drag his gun from his holster. Poole swore again, moved to his own Colt. He was very fast, and had drawn and pulled the trigger as Quirrel fell into him.

'I stuck him with a muck fork. You even got that wrong,' Poole said with disgust.

'No!' shouted Nibbs, as the gunshot boomed, blunted and fatal.

Quirrel didn't make a sound other than a short grunt before falling at Poole's feet.

The Chinaman drew out a short-barrelled revolver, then shot Nibbs twice as he shook his head, holding out his hands. Poole stepped away, tried to see what the barman, or any one else was going to do.

He yelled for Chumser, trod on Quirrel's head in his haste to get out. He punched his way through the door, stared into the empty street. Chumser wasn't there, nor were the horses. But someone was and they hit him, hard.

Sheriff Morgan Kinney flinched, sucking in his breath as he smashed the picket post into the top side of Poole. Then he made a grab for the Colt as it fell from Poole's numb hand. Inside the saloon, the Chinaman swung his gun around. He was searching for a small-town brave man, but there wasn't one; only the barman with a scattergun pointed at him. 'You smile once more, you pig-tailed scum, and I'll make two o' you,' the man said.

Kinney pushed Poole in through the door. 'You see what happened here, Lem?' he demanded of the barman.

'Yeah, I saw it. Chester went for his gun. But he's drunk some . . . didn't have a chance. Your man Nibbs was murdered, plain an' simple.'

Kinney swore silently. 'Stupid . . . fatally stupid,' he said. He looked threateningly at Poole and the Chinaman as he considered his next move. 'I'll get these two behind bars, then I'll send a wire to Newburg. I'll ask for Will Mitten. He aint goin' to believe this.'

Poole straightened, his words were slow and painful. 'Why'd you come here?' he asked. 'Where's Chumser? I told him to . . . .'

'. . . .wait out front.' Kinney finished the sentence for him.' A man holdin' onto three horses? That's kind of interestin'. Keeps lawmen like me alive,' he said grimly.

As Kinney prodded them from the saloon, Poole turned and cast a low, withering look behind him.

The barman was watching him. He shrugged and muttered. 'I've forgotten you already.'

4

A Bad Deck

Trade was good, and the Horse Creek Stage Line had recently bought a Concord coach. It was a big, rugged model designed for frontier trade. It hadn't been long from the New Hampshire factory where its doors had been painted with individual scenes of rivers and mountains. Below the luggage deck a mud-spattered sign read, "Eagle Spring – Newburg".

The coach was grunting and groaning soundly, rocking easy on its braces behind the team of six strong bays. Inside there were four passengers. Four men sat up on the deck.

Three of them sat at the rear, facing forward. The two smaller men each had a wrist manacled to the deck rail. The larger man had a shoulder wound. He wore his right arm in a sling, and it was secured by a wrist iron and a short length of chain. Pick Hammond sat forward, his back to the driver's box. He was vigilant, and held a Winchester across his knees.

In the boot, beneath the driver's box was an iron, ring-bolted chest. There was a plate on top. It was engraved, "VQ Mining Co".

Seated next to the driver, Will Mitten had a look at the heavy leaden sky. Then he turned and glanced back at the prisoners, and doubted he'd go to the trouble of hauling canvas over their heads when the rain came.

'Careful boys. Marshal's got his eye on us ... thinks we might escape,' the injured man mocked painfully.

Will sniffed and spat loudly, then turned away. He didn't want to look at the man. He thought of the grin on Franklin Poole's face when he'd walked into the Eagle Spring jail. The two men had even shared an edgy reminiscence. But Will told Poole not to expect any favours from a US Marshal – it was customary to get chained to the deck if there was more than one prisoner, and if there were passengers.

Now seated on the box beside Will, Huck Ambler flicked the reins. The coach heaved in its braces and one of the two lady passengers whooped with excitement. Huck pointed the whip towards the peaks of the Sangre de Cristos where dark cloud masses were forming.

'That aint a pretty sight, Marshal,' he said. 'We'd best get to Blushing Lode. Take a look at the creek.'

Will nodded thoughtfully. Before they'd started out from Eagle Spring that morning, he knew full well that more rain could prevent them from going on. There'd been broken rain for three days, but it had been building. The evening before, they'd got the storm that had run the creeks and gullies to overflowing. The telegraph line to Newburg had been knocked down; that was why he'd chanced taking his prisoners straight off. He'd wired back to Newburg on Saturday, told them he'd be on the Monday stage. So they'd be waiting for him, especially Valentine Quirrel and old Bewle Callister.

It wouldn't took good if he didn't arrive. There'd be many folk carefully watching every move he made, what he did, how he did it. He knew that in the case of any other prisoner with such a wound, he'd have cuffed the wrist of his good arm. They'd even have rode inside the coach. But he couldn't do that with Franklin Poole.

The Eagle Spring – Newburg run was just short of sixty miles, and normally the coach would have made it in eight hours. Out of town, there was a ten-mile, hard-dipping stretch that gave Huck Ambler a chance to take his mind off driving the team. He could sit back, think up things to say.

'Yessir, Company owed me time,' he said, speaking above the snap of leather, the creak of ash. 'I'd been fishin' along the North Fork. Just got back this mornin' . . . heard what happened.' He paused for effect, then added, 'Chester Quirrel shot dead an' Jabber Nibbs too.'

'Yeah,' Will said. It was Jabber Nibbs who wanted to be Morgan Kinney's deputy in Eagle Spring.

21

Kinney had told Will that if Quirrel hadn't been on a whiskey soak with the aspirant deputy, if he hadn't caught the name 'Poole', he'd never have gone for his gun. He'd still be alive; they both would be.

'I reckoned this Poole feller got both of 'em,' Huck said.

'No, it was Quirrel, he killed. Reckon it was his way of keepin' the balance,' Will said. 'The Chinaman shot down Nibbs. But don't let him fool you: his heart's as black as that goddamn pigtail he wears.'

'How'd you mean "keepin' the balance"?' Huck asked.

'Frank Poole's notion of right an' wrong,' Kinney replied.

Huck knotted his brow, had a quick glance over his shoulder. 'Who's the other one, then?' he asked after a few moments.

'His name's Charlie Chumser, an' he aint much of a size either,' the marshal said. 'He's formed some sort o' partnership with Poole that I didn't ask about. But he aint done much I can nail him with. Maybe I'll let him go.'

'When did you get over from Newburg?' Huck wanted to know next.

'I got the news late Thursday night. Caught the stage next mornin',' Will told him.

'You're takin' them up to Fort Scott?'

'Yeah. We'll all be on tonight's train out of Newburg.'

Huck shook his head. 'Why'd he want to kill Chester Quirrel? There's others he could o' chose.'

'If you don't believe in coincidence or that "balance" I was talkin' of, I reckon doin' harm must be in his blood,' Will said. 'Nine years ago . . . maybe ten, he killed Louis Callister. You weren't around then.'

'I *was*. It was just a long way south o' here,' Huck said and glanced sideways. He had more questions to ask, but decided to stay quiet for a while. Huck liked and respected Will Mitten, and thought he understood some of the predicament. The agent at the coach station had told him that Franklin Poole had been a childhood friend of the marshal's.

Five minutes later, Will broke the uncomfortable silence. 'You know Cornfields Store, in Newburg?' he asked Huck.

'Yessir. Got me Sunday duds there,' Huck said.

'Remember an old timer, used to bag up nails . . . seeds an' stuff?'

Huck thought for a moment, then nodded. 'Yeah, I think so.'

'Well he's dead now,' Will said. 'He was Rimmer Poole, Frank an' me's pa – sort of. He weren't always a storeman. He was an army post trader . . . went bust. Him an' my ma knew each other pretty good. Came up from Utah to work a mine at Blushing Lode – a Quirrel mine. But he got ill . . . couldn't carry on minin'. He walked to Newburg, settled for a job at Cornfields. Ma died of the flux when me an' Frank weren't hardly into double figures.'

'What did you do?' Huck asked, after what he thought was a respectful silence.

Will made up a thin grin. 'Me an' Frank did some

23

fast growin'. Tried freightin', cuttin' wood for the Quirrel mines. We punched cattle for the Callisters even. If you worked, it was for one o' *them*. Frank stayed on, but I drifted up to Eagle Spring an' really grew up. Worked as a full-time deputy.'

'What happened to your real ma an' pa?'

'Don't know much about it. They were religious folk. Scoops, they called 'em. Got killed for it,' Will said coldly. 'Me an' Frank were only nubbins. It was Rimmer Poole an' Peggy Mitten found us . . . kind o' had one each. Gave us names.'

There was some more of the awkward silence, but the story was new to Huck and he was thrilled. 'What happened to Poole, after he killed Callister?' he asked tentatively.

'He did what any self-respectin' killer would do: took to the hills. Never heard of him again 'til that message came through from Morgan Kinney.'

All that was about as much talk as Huck Ambler had ever heard from the marshal. Huck reckoned he'd have continued, but they were close to the first relay station. Within minutes they saw smoke rising through a birch stand that bent around the station cabin. When they turned into the small clearing they heard the first booming grumble of thunder.

As Huck set the brake, the station manager's two boys were already at work unhitching the lead horses. Huck climbed down from the box, but Will didn't move.

'There's hot coffee waitin' for you all in the cabin,' Huck called.

From the driver's box, Will noticed the rain clouds were scudding north-east toward the Colorado border. From below and behind him, the coach door swung open and he heard the passengers talking as they disembarked.

He nodded at Pick Hammond, the deputy that Kinney had sent along. 'Go get your feed. When you're done, bring back somethin' for *them*,' he instructed.

As he took Hammond's Winchester, he turned and looked down, and saw that the passengers were looking up. There was the air of threat, of vital danger and they wanted to see the prisoners' faces.

'You'd think there was some other way of taking them to Newburg,' he heard one of the two young women say. 'They look more bestial than ever, chained up like that.'

'Howdy there, Ma'am,' Poole called out. 'I just know'd you got a pretty face under that bonnet.'

'Yeah, an' I'm pretty out of sorts, too,' Coral Keane muttered to herself. She lifted her skirts away from the cloying mud. It was just an inch or so more than was necessary, and the marshal held back a tolerant smirk.

'You get them to take this chain off, an' I'll be glad to carry you, Ma'am,' Poole called out.

'Please go straight to the cabin,' Huck said. 'We're losin' time. There's only twenty minutes while we get teams changed.'

Huck watched the passengers drag their feet across the mud as he returned to stand by the near-side wheel. He'd been talking to one of the station boys. 'The water's still a foot below the stringers at Blushing Lode,' he told Will. 'Well it *was* at noon, apparently. Do you want me to bring you somethin'? Coffee?'

The marshal shook his head. He knew now they'd be going on. He turned to face the men who sat unmoving against a sullen and threatening sky. The US Marshal was very uneasy and his heart pounded, but he stared hard and impassive at his prisoners.

5

The Decision

Frank Poole was wearing a dark, store-bought suit and he'd got his hat pulled forward so that it covered the top part of his face. But his eyes were bright, and they glinted and flicked with the prospect of a break.

None of the captives had given anything away. The Chinaman looked any age between fifteen and fifty, and there wasn't much more that Will knew about him. He'd looked into the man's dark eyes, and seen the badness. With Morgan Kinney, he'd gone through dodgers issued in El Paso and Santa Fe. They'd found one that had originally been issued by the Southern Pacific Railroad. It looked like their man; an Oriental, who'd robbed, killed and moved on without ever giving a name.

As for Chumser, Will would have let him go if it had been up to him. He'd done nothing more than hold the horses outside the River Bend Saloon when

Poole had gone in with the Chinaman and asked about his surrogate pa.

At first it had seemed strange to Will that Poole had risked coming back into New Mexico, let alone Eagle Spring, a mere sixty miles from Newburg. But he'd thought about it, and knew that Poole didn't need the intelligence, or to ask about any enemy's ordnance before going into battle.

But right now, Will knew what was on Poole's mind. The man was looking to escape, hoping for an edge – and was going to make one if he could.

Then, still far to the west, Will saw a sharp sliver of light. It was a spark of lightning and he knew that was their weakness. If it should rain now, and hard, they wouldn't get through. They'd be stranded, or have to spend the night at one of the relay stations.

'Hey, Marshal,' Chumser said suddenly. 'I need the can.'

Will looked up. It was something he'd been expecting. 'An' I need Mr Hammond to come back before any o' you go anywhere,' he said.

'I'm tellin' you, Marshal. I'm that full o' piss, I'll fill your drivin' box if I don't get rid of it now,' Chumser repeated.

Will ignored him. He waited for Pick Hammond, who carried out sandwiches and some coffee mugs balanced on a wooden platter.

'I brought you some anyway,' he said, handing a tin mug up to Will.

Will winked and took the coffee, placing it on the box beside him.

Then Hammond unshackled Chumser while Will held the Winchester on the other two. As Hammond went off with Chumser, Will asked the Chinaman if he was so inclined, but the man's face remained unreadable. Poole didn't even look up.

When Hammond and Chumser returned, Will got down from the box and took his coffee to the cabin. When he went in, one of the two businessmen was asking Jessica Dorne, the youngest of the two women, if she wanted some whiskey in her coffee. She said no, in a way that made it clear to Will that she wasn't a companion of Coral Keane. She said nothing more, and sat at the table with her cup of coffee clasped comfortingly in her hands. From her affronted look it was obvious that, although she was tolerating the two businessmen, she was also tired of them.

Both men glanced at Will as he approached, then nodded apprehensively. Will placed his empty coffee mug on the table, and let his eyes meet Jessica's.

'We've been talking to the driver,' she said, looking towards Huck. 'Since there's enough room, we wanted to ask if the man with the wounded arm could ride inside.'

Will smiled. 'There's nothin' in the rules to stop you from askin', Ma'am.'

'We really wouldn't mind,' Coral joined in.

'No, I just bet you wouldn't,' were the words Will didn't respond with. Instead he shook his head. 'Sorry, Ma'am. I appreciate your concern, but it can't be done,' he said. His voice sounded like the last word, and it wasn't questioned.

Will was the last to leave the cabin. When he did, the lead horses were being hitched. He glanced around him, before noticing that Poole and Chumser were alone on the coach deck. He swore, using Hammond's name badly and in vain, then calmed. The Eagle Spring deputy hadn't known that the Chinaman didn't want to take a leak. He didn't know not to take his eyes off Poole when Will wasn't there, ever. Hammond was a lawman and it hadn't seemed necessary for Will to tell him.

As Will walked faster to the coach he gripped his Colt, and saw that Poole was watching him. He wondered if the Chinaman had changed his mind, or had Poole had changed it for him. What the hell were they up to? Now he sensed Poole's hole card – the alternative to a chain and guns. And hadn't he already used some of his wretched charm on the women?

Huck was standing a little away from the coach, watching new thunderheads developing. Will knew then what was happening. Poole too had seen the storm clouds, and knew that every minute of delay would count against their making Newburg. For him, another minute against his eventual date with the gallows.

'Pick! Pick Hammond!' Will shouted.

The two station boys were almost finished with the lead-team hitch. Huck picked up on the mood and hollered for everyone to board. Then he climbed up on the box.

'You keep an eye on those prisoners,' Will told

him, above the noise of the hammering and then the gun shot. He cursed loudly, drew his Colt and started running. He ran around the horse sheds, towards the stand of birch where the privvies for the stage passengers were. Hammond was banging on one of the doors with the butt of his gun. 'He aint comin' out,' he yelled. 'Goddamn John China's got the door bolted.'

'The door's bolted?' Will echoed angrily. 'How'd you let that happen?'

'How was I supposed to stop him – go in there with him?' Hammond yelled back, 'What was that shot I heard?' Will asked.

'I was tryin' to scare him out.' Hammond pointed to the splintered hole, high in the privy door. 'It'd be way above his head.' He banged on the door again. 'You think he's OK? Not fallen in? He ain't a lofty man, Marshal.'

'If he has, you can ride downwind of him,' Will snapped. 'Stand back.'

When Will had kicked in the privvy door, they dragged out the Chinaman. He didn't resist or fight, just made insolent, slow progress. Hammond had to drag him back to the coach. Will had to kick his legs to get him up and manacled to the deck rail again. By that time, they'd lost another quarter hour. The storm clouds were drawing in, getting ever closer. Will saw Poole look up, and caught sight of the scheming glint in his eyes.

Both men were thinking that, if the rain came,

fifteeen minutes could mean them not reaching
Newburg that night.

6

Going Forward

The river called Horse Creek rose in the Sangre de Cristos, then fell sharply through the timberline to Eagle Spring. From there on, it made its long decline to Newburg and beyond. First, through a broad canyon, then more leisurely across the flats. Before the water grew wide it was crossed three times by the coach and wagon road. The first was known as Blushing Lode Bridge because the deserted mining town was only a few miles to the south. Callister's Bridge was so-called because it was where the creek formed the southern boundary to the family ranch. The third or last bridge was called Bear Crossing, and was eight miles out of Newburg.

With the horses still fresh, the stage rolled swiftly down through the canyon. But Huck told Will that if the westbound stage had left Newburg on schedule, and got through, they were a tad overdue to meet up with it.

Travelling steady, the coach climbed along the canyon rim, then onto a low rising plain where cottontails scattered into the brush. From atop the coach they could see a long way, and Will asked Huck to bring the team to a halt. They'd wait for the Newburg stage travelling from Callister's Bridge, and find out if the road from there on was clear.

The incoming coach appeared momentarily. It was silhouetted at first, then took on colour and structure as it rushed towards them. The driver saw them and bellowed at his lead team, hauling back on the box with the reins.

Chubby Rafter was a great, hairy man and round just about everywhere. He had a relief driver alongside him. They'd had to stop several times and move debris aside, Chubby said. Other than that it had been fair make way. Though Chubby spoke to those riding up front, his reckoning eyes were on Frank Poole.

'Well,' Huck said, glancing up at the sky, 'Maybe you'll make it at Blushing Lode, maybe you won't. We got the worst of it ahead. Them bridges are lower set. We got to move on.'

'Look out at Callister's,' Chubby warned. 'The water's gettin' fast . . . been undercuttin' the bank south side.' He lifted a plump, gloved hand. 'Bon Voyage!' he shouted.

Both drivers released their wheel brakes and their eager teams set their shoulders, pitched into their collars.

*

About halfway to the Blushing Lode Bridge, it began to rain. They stopped, and Huck, Will and Hammond pulled on their ponchos. Hammond was told to draw a tarp over the prisoners. As the horses raced east, the sky steadily grew darker, and with the throaty race of the creek in their ears the rain increased. Thunder was rolling in, and to the north, lightning flickered.

When they arrived at Blushing Lode Bridge, Will got down, and had to walk ahead with a lantern. In the mean light he could see the bridge timbers running wet and gleaming. He waved the coach on as he walked out onto the bridge. They'd make it, but he could feel the support beams shudder as the current swirled and pummelled them. And Callister's Bridge was another twenty miles. From there the road swept through more open country, along the flats to Bear Crossing and Newburg.

Seconds ahead of the pulsating waves of thunder, great blinding bolts speared the sky and Huck called reassurances to the team. 'Jesus, if we aint in to the mother of all storms' he shrieked above the noise.

Will watched in awe as bright spectres of fire danced along the horizon, seeing the horses' bulging eyes and flattened ears as they ran in dread. Then the rain changed direction, came in low. It was full in the face as if the creek itself was being wrung up and pitched at them. Will was going to tell Huck that if it wasn't for the lightning, they wouldn't be able to see the road ahead. But he thought better of it, and settled into the terror of their flight.

Sparks streamed from the brake shoes as the coach made a bend in the road, the detail standing out sharp and bright. They sped past the Blushing Lode turn-off, and Will saw the landfall ahead of them. For the first time ever, Huck drew his great bull whip. As the coach lurched up, he cracked the long rawhide lash sharply over the leaders' ears. He held the reins taut and sawed at the bits, keeping the horses steady until they responded to him once again. They ran the nightmare for many more miles, until another searing flash lighted the dark, rain-pitted water ahead of them. The creek was level with the road, washing across the timbers of Callister's Bridge. Huck yelled an alarm, and using all his strength hauled back on the reins to stop the team.

Will was down and running with the lantern before the horses were halted. He'd seen that the water was actually churning in the depression between the road bed and the uprights of the bridge. He looked along the bank for a stake of some sort, and found a broken pine branch to use as a probe. There was just over a foot of water between the surface of the road and the floor timbers of the bridge.

Huck came running with the iron pry bar that they carried under the rear boot of the coach. He stabbed at the rock and shale at the roadside, squinted at the swirling water. As he did, the team began to rear and whinny, plunging against the brake.

Will stared frantically around him, wondering if they could still make it back to the Blushing Lode turn. Like Huck, he had been thinking that if they could get debris into the fill – and if they could do it fast enough – they'd get across the bridge, and reach the safety of the higher road beyond.

'Get everybody out of the coach,' Huck shouted above the rolling echo of thunder. 'I'll start prying stuff from the bank. Get 'em all out here – an' I mean all of 'em.'

For an instant Will hesitated, startled by the note of authority in Huck's voice – or was it panic? 'Not the prisoners. I'll get the others,' he said in response.

Huck took a step forward, grabbed his arm. 'You'd rather they drown?' he asked. 'And us along with 'em? I said to get 'em all . . . Marshal.'

Will puffed out his cheeks, turned and went back to the plunging horses and the coach. No way was he taking the chain away from Poole – not until he got him up to Fort Scott. He told Pick Hammond to release Chumser and the Chinaman, and get them down quick to help move rock. Then he pulled open the door of the coach. Someone had obviously been ill and the stench rolled out.

Will snorted with disgust, and gave them Huck's challenge. 'Driver tells me if you stay inside, we all drown. I ain't about to argue with him, so you ain't doin' it to me. We're makin' some civic improvements . . . and that's all o' you,' he barked.

*

Dirt and stones were easy to come by, tumbling readily from the rain-sodden bank. No one needed to have the threat made clear, and Huck worked furiously with the pry bar. The two women and the businessmen hurriedly picked up rubble to pack in the fill.

Huck was the one who'd be driving near two tons of coach and cargo across the fill onto the bridge, so he'd decide when they'd done enough. But the level of the water was rising fast, and it was clear there were only a few more minutes in which to get it done.

Will watched as Huck stepped onto the fill-in and started to poke about with his bar. Then the sky flashed, broke apart again and he turned to look at the team. The horses had already started to slew the coach around and he rushed forward. Huck yelled out, but his voice was lost as the thunder crashed down.

Will turned back for a second. He saw Huck was down, propping himself up on his arms as the water rushed around him and over the bridge. He had one leg doubled uneasily beneath him, the other was trapped in the fill.

One leg was broken below the knee, and Huck was near to drowning by the time Will got him dragged back on the road. Then, as Will turned to get help from Pick Hammond, he saw the Newburg deputy stretched out flat in the water that ran fast across the road. Will groaned, then swore as he reached for his gun. It was the Chinaman who was behind him, who whammed him in the head and the middle of his back with Hammond's Winchester.

Will Mitten fought against losing consciousness, and listened with detached fascination as the rumbling in his head overlapped the roaring of the water in the creek. He was lying in the road beside Huck, his gunbelt and gun taken from him. The Chinaman was standing a few feet away holding one of the lanterns and the Winchester. Chumser had another lantern, the carbine from the driver's box and Will's Colt, and was telling the passengers to get back in the coach.

'Hurry 'em up,' Poole shouted, 'then get this goddam chain off me. Someone look under the driver's box, see if there's any brown bottles.'

Will wondered who the 'someone' was. It sounded like Poole thought there might be some medicines on board – wanted something for the pain that racked his arm and shoulder. Will hoped there wasn't. That would be some good news, he thought, and turned his head. He saw that both Hammond and Huck were sitting up, and considered his chances as he stretched his fingers around a large flat stone.

The Chinaman seemed to smile fleetingly. Then he hoisted the Winchester and shook his head slowly.

'Hey Will,' Poole called out. 'You goin' to lie there all night? Let's get this sodden rig turned an' out o' here.'

As Will rose awkwardly to his feet, stumbling a

pace sideways, he saw the bridge was now impossible to cross. He stood steady, chewed on his lip. If it hadn't been for Huck, and the women, he'd have taken his chances with the Chinaman. But he was a US Marshal. Their safety came first.

'Let's get Huck out o' the road, and into the coach,' he said looking at Hammond.

The deputy got up slowly. He'd lost his hat and there was thin, bright blood running down his forehead. He stooped, grasped Huck under one arm and they lifted him. Huck made painful little hopping movements, but together they got to the coach, and Will manhandled him across the step. Huck gasped with pain at that moment, stared hard into Will's wrought face.

'I know, it hurts. If you were a horse I'd have to shoot you – so live with it,' the marshal said drily.

Poole was standing up on the deck with another coach lantern in his hand. The Chinaman had freed him with the keys he'd taken from Hammond.

'Get in the coach, Deputy,' Poole told Hammond. 'Will, you get on the box ... take the reins. Chumser!' he shouted, 'take a lantern and go stand thirty or forty paces back up the road.'

Chumser slid down the rear cargo boot into the ankle-deep water. Will, watched closely by the armed Chinaman, climbed up onto the box and untied the reins. Before he let the brake go he allowed the team a mighty strain against the stage pole. The Chinaman pulled himself onto the deck again and Poole dropped into his place beside Will. Out on the road,

Chumser waved his lantern as the coach started its way back towards Blushing Lode.

7

The Road Back

Will knew the stretch of road, and so did the horses. In the darkness, water surging up to their hocks, rain lashing against them, the bays laid back their ears and ran.

After fifteen miles or so, Will knew they had a good chance of making the Blushing Lode turn. But as they now got closer, there was a sound that worried him; a complementary note to the roaring of the creek. He soon realized that it was the sound of water rushing into the bend ahead of them, racing straight across the road and into the creek.

The water grew relentlessly deeper and swifter, and the team slowed. Sensing immediate danger, the horses fought the rising cross-flow run. Will realized that he should have cut the team loose back at the bridge, and let everyone make their own way to higher ground. For a second he'd let his mind wander, and was thinking how they'd have carted Huck when Poole jabbed his arm.

'The arroyo,' he shouted above the roar of the water.

Will shook his head clear. He knew right away what Poole meant. But he didn't think the horses or coach could make it. The wheels were no longer throwing out spray; they were turning slower in water that was axle-deep.

He whooped, cheered on the horses, cracked Huck's whip out into the menacing darkness. Up ahead, he could just make out the road where it widened, where the once-dry arroyo turned alongside the creek towards the bridge.

The arroyo was about a mile west of the Blushing Lode turn-off. When the town had been worked, riders who knew the country had used it as a short cut to the wagon road. Freighters would haul over to take a break, and let the stage through. But now the coach team was slipping and floundering in its harness. Will eased the horses forward, cursing as progress seemed impossible.

But the arroyo was going to help. Help as much, if not more, than when it ran dry. The torrent was deflecting the flooded creek. For the width of the road, it was displacing it with its own flow of water.

Will yelled himself hoarse, dragged savagely at the bit of the near-side leader, and turned the team into the mouth of the arroyo.

Will didn't really know why he'd made the turn. If

any wagon had ever hung to the margins of the arroyo all the way to Blur Lode, he'd never heard of it. But for the sake of taking charge of his prisoners once again, or the loss of ten lives, it didn't seem that he'd much to be beaten for.

He considered the coach, assessed its durability and strength. If any vehicle could make it, the Concord could. It wasn't constructed like a wagon or freighter. Thorough-braces took the shocks, freed the wheels from obstacles the moment they were met. This was good for the team, and didn't convey jolts and judders to them through the stage pole and its traces.

The torrent of water coming through the arroyo was all storm water. It was highly coloured and rising, but not yet wild enough to undercut the banks.

Frequently they dropped to a walk, the leaders picking their way along the bankside like a span of pack mules. But Will only had to stop once to back the team, drag the leaders around a rock fall. Then he upped the pace. Under the now slackening rain, he let them feel the let-up of his tension through the reins.

Then finally they ran from the arroyo, swung onto the track down to Blushing Lode. The horses sensed a stop, and ran willingly towards the deserted town.

'Some drive for a marshal, Will,' Poole said – just about the only words the two men had shared since Callister's Bridge.

Will took a deep breath, then gave a thin smile. 'You told the Chinaman to lock himself in that john?' he asked.

Poole laughed, but that was all.

'Yeah, I should o' guessed,' Will gritted.

A minute or so later, Poole said, 'Reckon I owe you for gettin' this coach through.'

'Yeah, reckon you do. Why mention it?'

'You'll find out,' Poole said.

Will thought the remark over for a while. 'They'll catch you,' he said. 'If Bewle Callister or old Quirrel have anything to do with it, they'll hunt you down an' cut your heart out. The law . . . *I*, won't protect you an' you know it. You won't be gone for ten years this time, Frank.'

'You should be worryin' about tonight, Will,' was Poole's response. 'You got more'n me in your charge.'

'The women deserve somethin' for their work at Callister's Bridge,' Will said pointedly. 'One of 'em can tend to Huck's leg . . . if they haven't already. There'll be some sort of stablin' I hope for the horses. Every one else can sleep in the saloon if it's still there.'

Poole grunted. 'It's still there. There's even a stove,' he said.

'You been here?' Will was surprised.

'Yeah, last Tuesday night,' Poole said. 'I didn't know the town had died. We came down through the timberline, used the old road. Got here just after sundown. Just wind blowin' the tumbleweed. Not a soul. No ghosts. Not a mad dog even.'

Riding down into Blushing Lode, Will understood Poole's feelings. It was where they'd spent early years as close as brothers. But that was something that had died, died without a burial.

'You been up here recently?' Poole asked him.

'Two years ago. Callister's had some horses stolen. Everyone expected whoever done it would come from around here.'

'Callister,' Poole echoed sneeringly. Then he said, 'Old Bewle's still alive then?'

'Oh yeah. He won't think o' dyin' now. Not until he sees you in the ground,' Will replied. 'He's been offerin' a thousand dollars for your hide all these years. That won't have changed.'

Now, as they approached the little town, the storm abated and holes of inky blue appeared through the dark overcast sky. Then the moon sailed free, and the bleached remains of the old houses and mine buildings shone like small piles of bones.

Will turned the coach at the bottom of the long slope, around the gaunt structures of a stamp-mill and boarding house. The horses with their coats hot and steaming trotted up the single street until Will halted them out front of Sapper Hole.

A last, fading gust of storm wind brushed along the street. It unsettled some tin from outbuildings, rattled loose shingles, slammed doors. From somewhere a windmill whirred above a well that it had long ago pumped dry. For a few more moments a frail, eerie life ran through the town. Then it passed and Poole stood up on the box.

'Will,' he said, 'looks like we got home.'

Will wrapped the reins around the brake and looked behind him, stared into the barrel of the Chinaman's rifle.

'Get down,' Poole said. 'You and that deputy get the driver inside, and see about unhitchin' the team.'

8

Blushing Lode

The door of Sapper Hole had been boarded up, but despite the sign which said, 'Property of VQ Mining Co. – No Trespassing', the planks had long since been wrenched off. They'd been burned up in the stove by passers-through. Others had graffitied rebellious messages across the sign itself. Some writers had given old Valentine Quirrell more personal, pithy proposals about what he could do with his mine and the town.

Guarded by the Chinaman, Poole ordered the women and the two businessmen into the saloon. He and Chumser covered Will and Hammond while they helped to take Huck in. Then, with guns still on them, the captive lawmen unhitched the team and led the horses into the stable, bringing feed oats from the rear boot. When they were through, the same guns were held to their backs while they were handcuffed.

In the bar room, only one wagon-wheel chandelier, a part section of the bar and the stove remained.
To get wood for the stove, the passers-through who'd
taken shelter had hacked pieces from the bar, razed
interior walls. Other than that, only the whiff of
whiskey and the sour, aged reek of beer remained.

Using Poole's chain, Will and Pick Hammond
were secured to an upright timber, each with one
hand left free. Leaving the Chinaman on guard,
Poole went back to the coach with Chumser.

Through the saloon door, Will could just make out
the coach standing in the moonlit street, and could
see Chumser in the front boot with a lantern. He
heard the excited shout when Chumser discovered
the VQ Mining Company chest.

'If only I hadn't taken my eyes off that Chinaman,'
Hammond said.

Will shook his head slowly. 'It aint all down to you,
Pick. I'm thinkin' there's been a few slip-ups that I'm
responsible for.'

Will sat quiet and rueful, watching Poole return
with the axe that had been strapped to the rear of the
coach. The man went over to where the dishevelled
and scared businessmen were sitting on the port-
manteaus they'd carried in. He asked one of them
his name.

'Stammer. George Stammer,' the man said.

'Well Mr Stammer, we can't have you restin' up
just yet. There's work to be done. Go chop some
wood and start a fire,' Then Poole threw a challeng-
ing look at the other man.

'Lovecraft,' the man said without being asked.

Poole looked slightly amused. 'Go help bring stuff in from the coach,' he told him. Then he asked Huck, 'Who can unlock the treasure chest?'

'With keys – Valentine Quirrel,' Huck replied directly.

Poole laughed, just as Stammer swung the axe at the remainder of the bar. He blinked irritatedly, and turned to the women.

Jessica Dorne was sitting on the carpet bag she'd been carrying on the coach. Coral Keane had thrown off her hat and sodden cloak, and stood with her hands on her hips. Neither of them looked scared, only fatigued by what they'd gone through. They didn't say anything, but carefully watched Poole.

Lovecraft staggered in with a sack of foodstuff he'd got from the coach. There were molasses, flour, bacon, coffee and some canned peaches. They were provisions that were meant to be offloaded at the relay station, but for one reason or another, Huck had forgotten. Lovecraft put the sack down near the stove, turned and went back out.

'We'll build us a fire,' Poole said, 'then we'll all eat. There's a spring pipe out back, ladies. Make yourselves useful and make coffee.'

Poole glanced around the room at the others; at Will, Hammond, Huck and Stammer who'd made some kindling. 'Don't any of you think about runnin' off. You're safe enough here, but you won't be out there,' he laughed.

'I don't want to be running off anywhere,' Coral

said. 'I like it just fine here.' She brushed past Stammer. 'You bring the wood,' she told him. 'I'll tend the stove.' She looked teasingly across at Poole. 'I only wish there was some bottled stuff behind the bar instead of the yellow man,' she said.

But along with the food provisions, there was a keg of what they called Pass wine in the front boot of the coach. Chumser found it, brought it in and set it up on what was left of the bar, then knocked out the bung.

Drawing deep on a cigarette, swallowing his brandy, Will thought back over the day, and considered the errors he'd made.

'You figgerin' what they're up to?' Pick Hammond quietly asked him.

The marshal fixed his eyes on Jessica Dorne as she fried off some bacon. Coral was making flour and corn dough in a pot.

'Yeah, that's *exactly* what I been doin',' Will said haplessly. 'I figure they're goin' to belly strap some o' the bays ... give 'em somethin' to hang on to. They'll try an' break out – go up through the timberline to the border.' The marshal sighed, swallowed more brandy, built another cigarette.

Lovecraft suggested to Poole that they have a look at Huck's fractured leg. He'd got some medical experience, he said. Not much, but better than nothing. 'I got to cut the boot off. I'll need a knife ... a sharp one,' he asked.

Will was sure someone carried a knife, but he kept

quiet. The same thought didn't seem to occur to Poole and he handed over his own pocket knife. Then Poole walked over to Will. After a moment he shifted his tin cup, grasped it with the fingers that stuck out from his sling. 'Don't suppose you ever considered this development, did you Will?' he asked.

'No,' Will confessed, 'I never did.' He took another pull on his brandy, and caught sight of the rope as he drained the cup.

Bleached and dusty, the rope angled up from a pegged cleat on the side wall near to him. It ran to a pulley hanging from the timber-beamed ceiling. From the rope, a flat wagonwheel was suspended: a makeshift chandelier that could be raised and lowered to light or extinguish its lamps.

But Poole's attention was elsewhere. He was listening beyond the stillness of the saloon. It was, and Will knew too, the sound of the fast-rising water of the arroyo as it raced around the perimeter of the town.

'The mine-road bridge won't get washed out – not with that iron rig for support,' Poole said decisively.

'Sure, you'll get across the bridge,' Will said. 'Even get into the foothills. But you'll never make the border. When we don't show up at Newburg tonight, they'll send riders.'

Poole looked attentively at Will as he continued.

'Think about it, Frank. First thing in the mornin', Quirrel and Callister'll get a posse together. An' they won't be ridin' coach horses bareback, either. When they get to you, as they surely will, they'll turn into a lynch mob . . . if you're lucky.'

Poole gave him a wily grin. 'I *am* thinkin' about it,' he said. 'I'm also thinkin' it's mighty discomfortin' for you to be caught like this. Yessir, I'm thinkin' it's their money keeps you goin', Will. That's what's really worryin' you – more than what's goin' to happen to me.'

'Think what you like, Frank. I'm just tellin' you what I know.'

Poole grinned again. 'What would *you* do?'

Will shook his head slowly. He knew he'd do the same – make a run for it – and Poole knew it too.

Poole went on with his thoughts. 'They're goin' to think you rigged it . . . set this up for my escape. Aces back to back, Will. You wearin' the chain an' all. They'll have you for how it looks.'

'Maybe. What I do know is, it'll be me that tracks you down, Frank. Me that brings you in. You'll never have a decent sleep as long as you live.'

'Maybe I should put a bullet in you right now?' Poole remarked drily.

'Maybe you should Frank. From what's been said about young Louis Callister, and now Chester Quirrel, I've just about got the advantage that suits you.'

'Don't get me excited, Will,' Poole said. Then he asked, 'Why'd you really want to track me down . . . bring me back? It ain't because you think I should hang. I know you too well.'

'I'm a US Marshal. I'm paid to get you to Fort Scott to stand trial.'

'OK, so we both got to worry about Quirrel an' Callister. But you got to ask yourself this Will: are they worth it?'

9

Holed Up

Poole had sat near Coral, watching her as he ate. When he'd finished, he got Chumser to pour him two cups of aguardiente, and gave one of the to the girl.

Her hair was awry and she was mud-spattered and tired, but she was a handsome woman, Will thought. She was sitting on George Stammer's portmanteau. Poole hunkered down, facing her.

'What would someone who looks like you want in a nasty old place like Newburg?' he asked her.

'Yeah. I can see how you'd be interested,' she told him. 'Particularly when I'm looking an' feeling like a pot chicken. I do a variety turn, Mr Poole. I was playing an engagement up in Raton, when I was introduced to Jaap Pin. If you didn't know already, he owns a saloon and dance hall in Newburg. He prevailed on me to accept an engagement. *That's* what I want in that nasty ol' place.'

'What do you *do*, in your variety act?' Poole asked. Will couldn't tell whether it was with genuine or time-killing interest.

'You'll have to come and see,' Coral said with a significant smile.

Then Chumser made a move towards Jessica Dorne. His eyes rolled and he wiped the back of a greasy hand across his mouth. He said something to her, but she didn't answer. Instead, she looked directly at Will, then came over to him.

'Would you like some more coffee, Marshal?' she asked.

'No thank you,' he said.

'I'm sorry for what happened,' she said. 'It is going to look bad for you, isn't it?'

'Yeah, but I'll live.' Will saw that they were being closely watched.

'Don't talk,' Poole called to the girl. He got up and came over. 'Don't go talkin' to the prisoners,' he requested.

'Don't be so dramatic,' the girl protested. 'I just asked if he wanted more coffee. We weren't planning a breakout,' she huffed and moved away.

'Can you take on any more o' that brandy?' Poole inquired of Will.

Will was already feeling woozy, and didn't want to get a bad head. But he thought maybe he'd get Poole drunk, or have a try. It could be to his advantage, although dangerous, he knew. 'Yeah, reckon I got the taste for it,' he said. 'An' we can't leave it for any incomers or no-goods to get their bellies around.'

Poole called to Chumser for him to bring the barrel over, and winced as he tried to make himself more comfortable on the floor. 'Did you know they tried to track me down before?' he asked.

'Yeah, I heard.'

'I met up with the men they sent, in Alicande. They were hired killers . . . both of 'em. One of 'em talked a bit, just before he died . . . mentioned the name Callister. That don't make the bigtime rancher much worse than me, does it Marshal?'

'When you killed Louis, you killed the only Callister heir,' Will said. 'There's only Bewle now, and he won't be content with a just an' proper hangin'.'

'Yeah, you already said. Eat my heart out, weren't it'?'

Will could tell that the brandy had worked some way on Poole. He watched as the man turned around to see whose attention he held; knew it was a sure sign he was losing it.

'I killed Callister in a fair fight,' Poole said more loudly. 'What was *wrong*, was that *he* was a Callister an' I was sweet on a lass that *he* wanted . . . that a *Callister* wanted.'

Poole took a drink from his cup, and stared hard at Will again. 'You punched cattle for the Callisters – same as me.' he said. 'You remember? Beef, chickory, a dollar a day and no future. Try an' set up on your own and they'd kill you. That or leave the country. We weren't born here Will, but we spent a near life-time on the land, goddammit.'

Will was touched by Poole's loathing for things

Callister. He knew it was the truth that sparked the feeling and he said nothing, deciding to let memories do their own dirty work.

'It weren't right, Will,' Poole said. 'The Callisters wanted to own everything, even us. Jesus, I thought we were supposed to have done with slavery . . . had a war for it.'

Will nodded wretchedly. 'They started out just like you an' me, Frank,' he said, without any real meaning or side.

'Started out from Utah, maybe,' Poole muttered, 'but they were *never* like me. I killed two men in fair fights. Fair from where I was. *That's* what I'm guilty of, an' for *that* they'd hang me. For *that* you'd hunt me down. Why, Will? For God's sake, why?'

'Because I'm sworn.'

'No, it aint for that, Marshal Will Mitten, an' you know it.'

'There's the would-be deputy,' Will reminded him. 'Maber Nibbs.'

'It was the Chinaman shot him. We're talkin' about me. No, it's about a Callister then a Quirrel. They're the ones that pinned that badge on you, an' they're the ones who're goin' to take it away,' Poole shouted. Then he turned to face the others.

'Valentine Quirrel owned this town,' he told them. 'Still owns what's left of it. He owned the people too. You paid rent to Quirrel and traded at his store. Most everybody who worked in his mines were in debt to him. He never paid enough for you to be anythin'

58

else. If you made a dollar clear, he'd find a way to get it from you.'

Will heard him, and from his own experiences knew again it was the truth.

Poole was less strident now, and sounded more tired, done in. 'My old man might o' died in a store in Newburg,' he told them, 'but it was a Quirrel mine that killed him – the rock dust in his lungs. They carried your pa home one night after he tried to stop some o' Quirrel's men shootin' each other. You remember Will? They shot *him* instead.'

Will said nothing. He took a swallow of brandy. Then his chain clanking faintly in the silence, he set his cup down and rolled another cigarette.

'What's in that chest's ours,' Poole told him with quiet fervour. 'It's what our pa's earned and never got. It's ours by right.'

'That's crazy talk, Frank,' Will told him, but with an unmistakable touch of doubt. 'Anyways, it's a strongbox . . . built to resist you.'

'It ain't *that* strong, Will. There's somethin' old Quirrel forgot,' Poole said slowly.

'Oh yeah, what's that then, Frank?'

Poole snickered. 'You'll find out,' he said. 'Right now we're goin' to catch some sleep . . . most of us.' His words were slurred and very weary.

10

The Hanging Wheel

Charlie Chumser had drawn first watch. He stretched out on the remains of the bar, propped himself on an elbow. For company, he had the carbine and a big stem-winder he'd borrowed from Huck Ambler.

Poole had topped up his and Huck's cup with brandy, then punched the bung back in the keg. Him and the Chinaman were now asleep, as were the dead beat Stammer and Lovecraft. Huck was quietly drunk, sometimes mumbling, sometimes grunting and growling. Newburg's Deputy Pick Hammond also slept fitfully, now and again snoring loud.

From a corner of the room, where they lay on a heavy, coach blanket, Will could hear the women's voices. He smiled to himself. Coral Keane, he thought, would be the one most used to not sleeping. He heard her say to Jessica Dorne, 'You asleep yet, honey?' Then she said, 'Listen, I said why I was going to Newburg – how about you?'

'I don't like being told who to marry . . . who not to. The excessive burden of family,' Jessica told her after a moment's consideration.

'Yeah, who'd have 'em,' Coral carelessly agreed.

Then their voices lowered and Will thought he heard Coral mention Poole. Correctly, he guessed they were weighing up their predicament. If he'd been in Poole's boots, he would have fed and rested the horses a couple of hours, then been on his way. But Poole acted as if he had time, and slept as if his troubles were behind him. The more Will thought about Frank Poole the more baffled he was by him.

In the meantime, while pretending to sleep, he leaned back against the timber stud. He'd been thinking about the rope and the wagonwheel chandelier. If it fell on a man, hit him squarely, it would no doubt kill him. Even a glancing blow would disable him, crack a few bones. He wouldn't mind killing the Chinaman, if he could get him underneath it, then he'd get the Winchester if he moved fast enough. But the chain that held him was wrapped around the stud and had Pick Hammond on the other end of it. Anyway, if he was going to do it, he'd have to wait; wait for the Chinaman, then somehow lure him, get him to move.

After an hour, Chumser's eyelids were drooping. In the low light, Will saw him ease himself down from the bar and walk over to the door. Chumser looked across at the coach then he slowly came back, stopped and stared down at Lovecraft's boots. He picked one up and examined it, measured it against one of his own feet. He decided they'd fit him, sat down and exchanged them for his own scuffed and shabby footwear.

Will chuckled silently, glad he hadn't fallen asleep. Hammond gave a violent snore and woke himself up. Will nudged him, and when he was fully awake, told him what he'd been thinking. He whispered that all the timbers were insecure, dried-out and half-rotten. He was sure a combined lunge against the chain would break them free.

'How you figurin' to get that Chinaman to stand just where you want him? He ain't like us . . . don't do what you'd expect. They got their own language,' Hammond said intriguingly.

'I know – haven't thought it through properly yet,' Will said. 'I just wanted to give you the chance to say "no" to doin' it, if you wanted.'

While Hammond thought about it, they both watched Chumser who, having stolen Lovecraft's boots, was now opening the man's case which had been thrown down from the deck of the coach. He pulled out a small book, then turned the first few pages in a confused way. Then he placed it carefully back in the case, and turned back to the bar.

'I hope *he* don't get in the way when we go for it,' Hammond said quietly, nodding towards Chumser.

'Yeah, so do I,' Will said and grinned.

Chumser was looking hard at the stem-winder when Will asked him what time it was. But he didn't rise to the test, just went over and woke the Chinaman.

The Chinaman uttered menacing sounds, and was awake like a rattled copperhead. Then he rolled up on to his feet, and Chumser snugged down in his place.

The Chinaman glanced at the marshal and the deputy. He moved over to the door and picked up a lantern, then went and looked at the women.

'He sure scares the marrow out o' me,' Will said. He'd got his knife out, held it down by his leg. 'Hey,' he called out.

The Chinaman turned to look at him, the lantern hardly lighting the chill of his black eyes.

'Water,' Will said.

The Chinaman uttered a low, oriental curse and went over to the bar, hoisted himself up and lay flat.

The only sound then was the low growl of the arroyo as it rushed around the outskirts of the town. For a long minute Will listened, then he began again.

'Hey,' he called. He took his tobacco and papers from his shirt pocket and tossed them under the wheel. 'You understand water? You son of a malignant yellow bitch. I'll trade you them makin's for a cupful. I mean we ain't in short supply, you stinkin' sawn-off devil worshipper,' he added angrily and gratuitously.

He knew the Chinaman would want tobacco. He recalled seeing a big group of Chinamen who'd laid rail track for the Southern Pacific having their photograph taken at Yuma. With their pipes and cigarettes, they'd all stood still like smokestacks. He also knew the Chinaman would get pleasure from taking the tobacco and not giving water in return.

He watched as the man suddenly got interested and sat up, peering over at the sack of tobacco and book of papers. He knew, or rather hoped the Chinaman was unaware of the big heavy cartwheel that was hanging in the shadows above.

As the Chinaman carefully swung down off the bar, Will glanced at Hammond, and saw the gleam in the deputy's eyes as they met his. Hammond was ready though, and grasped the chain as Will's free hand produced the knife.

11

Breaking Up

When the Chinaman's feet hit the floor, he took one pace then stopped. Him, Will and Hammond heard the jangle of a bridle bit at the same time. It was close, and when a horse whinnied the Chinaman hissed out for Poole.

Poole was awake almost before the sound of his name had died. One moment he was apparently in his slumber, the next ducking low with Will Mitten's Colt in his hand. For a few seconds he listened to the sound of approaching horses, then indicated for the Chinaman to move back and cover Will and Hammond. Then Poole withdrew to the night shadows at the back of the bar.

The lawmen could see the look of hostility from the Chinaman, and could tell by his eyes they were dead men if they made a sound.

Now above the sounds of the horses, they heard

voices. Two riders appeared in the moonlit street, and rode past the coach before dismounting. Then they looked around them, then stepped uneasily up to the door of the saloon.

'Stop right there,' Poole greeted them. 'You're both perfectly framed, so I ain't goin' to miss.' Then as if on cue, the Chinaman took a few fast, threatening steps towards the silhouetted men.

Will gasped, and nudged Hammond. 'Now!' he said urgently, as the Chinaman got directly beneath the wheel. With his knife-hand extended, he lunged for the rope, and had nearly made it when the gunshot exploded through the carcass of the old building.

The rope parted when Will's knife hit it just above the cleat, and the stud nails screeched. Then with a great boom, the wheel crashed to the floor inside a circle of billowing dust. But in spite of the violent hurt in their wrists, the stud had held. The chain hadn't moved much, but the Chinaman had.

Poole leapt to his feet, shouting at Chumser who was running eagerly towards the door with the carbine. 'Let him go,' he yelled at him.

The Chinaman turned to stare down at the big, iron-bound chandelier. Then he looked over at Will. He saw the knife, the two men lunging desperately one more time against the chain. As he realized what was going to be his fate, the Chinaman's face tightened. He levered up another round, and again pulled the trigger of the Winchester. But Poole had got there and was on him, the bullet splintering a plank close to Will's feet.

Although injured, Poole was nearly double the size of the Chinaman. He brought his Colt barrel down hard and fast across the man's wrist and the Winchester clattered to the floor. The pain was too much for the Chinaman's mute bearing, the quality of his howl unnerving for everyone in the saloon.

Will groaned and swore. He slumped back wearily against the stud, and looked beyond Poole and the Chinaman to the body that lay face-down in the doorway.

'What Will says about you's only half the truth of it, you trigger-happy bastard. You didn't give 'em a chance,' Poole rasped. 'Then you never do, do you China?' he said as an afterthought.

The Chinaman shook his head indolently, pointed down at the man.

Will saw that the man's hands weren't going up. One of them was clasped to the butt of his drawn gun.

Poole looked uncomfortable. 'Get rid of the knife. Will,' he said. 'Throw it over here.'

Poole then gave Chumser the keys and told him to unlock the wrist irons. The chain rattled, fell around the stud and Will and Hammond were free again. But the Chinaman had reclaimed the Winchester, and breathing fast and shallow, levelled it in the crook of his arm. Will didn't know what to think; he couldn't figure out Poole's next move. He told Hammond to do as they said, to keep calm as the Chinaman prodded them to the doorway.

Chumser moved forward and turned the body over. He undid the man's gunbelt, and strapped it around his own waist and bent to take the gun. At the back of his mind, Will wondered who'd be providing the trousers and pants. Then he looked at the face of the man who stared lifeless into the blue, silvery moonlight. The man whose blood pooled glossy and black on the floor.

'You know him?' Poole asked.

'Will nodded. 'Yeah. It's Jale Stetter. He was a Callister foreman.'

'Who do you think the other one was?' Poole asked. 'What would they want here?'

'I don't know' Will said, impassively. 'Perhaps they were out lookin' for us.'

Poole winced at some sudden inner pain. He looked out the door at Stetter's saddle horse. 'We'll get the team hitched up, pronto,' he said.

'Hitch up the team?' Will echoed in measured surprise.

'Yeah, that's right. We're ridin' to Stonewall in style.'

'How you goin' to get there?' Will asked.

'Usin' the timber road.'

Will shook his head slowly, gazing at Poole. 'You taken a knock, Frank? You can't get a coach over *that* road, it's another devil's slide. Even if you could, riders would still catch you up.'

'Maybe. But there'll be two women in the coach. Hostages, Will, for our safe ride.'

Will stared at him and swore impulsively. For a

moment he looked at the Chinaman and Chumser, then he met Poole's gaze again. 'How you figurin' on takin' a six-horse hitch over that road with one good arm?' he asked calmly. 'Or do you think your gang of desperadoes can handle it?'

'No, don't reckon they can. That's why *you'll* be takin' the reins, Will. You made a mistake – showed us all how good you are.'

'We'll meet in Tophet first,' Will snarled.

'No again, Will. *First* you'll be drivin' us across the border . . . with or without a gun at your head. Then we'll see.' Poole brought up the Colt and his eyes were alive. He was confident again, thought he'd got a way out. 'Now move,' he ordered.

With the Chinaman's gun on them, Will could only consider their predicament. Him and Pick Hammond led the horses out, made up the hitch. As he tested the traces, the sense of Poole's daring proposal unfolded.

The women were crucial, he thought. A fired-up posse might doubt, but could they be sure that the two-time killer, Franklin Poole wouldn't kill Coral or Jessica Dorne if his escape was threatened? And it was true that up to a few years ago, all sorts of vehicles *had* passed over the timber road. Now, they were carrying shovels, axes, and another pry bar in the coach. There was still plenty left of the provender they'd forgot to drop at the relay station, and spare feed for the team. And then it hit him. Poole wouldn't be leaving behind Valentine Quirrel's iron-bound chest.

Will then understood what Poole had meant, when he'd said he owed him, for getting the coach through. When he'd said, 'you'll find out'. He understood why he'd had the luggage and other stuff removed. It was to lighten the load. Poole had got the idea of taking the coach back over the old timber road when they'd got through the arroyo. Poole had taken the same trail from the border country only a few days before. He knew the chances of making it all the way to Stonewall.

He didn't know how it would end, only that he had no choice. 'Better to drive than to be dead', his pa would probably have said. 'Where there's a will there's a way, son.'

When they'd made the hitch and tied Stetter's horse on behind, Will and Hammond were nudged back to the saloon. Stammer, Lovecraft, Coral and Jessica Dorne were being close herded by Chumser. They all looked pale, tired and somewhat fearful.

'What's goin' to happen to us?' Stammer asked nervously. 'You can't leave us here.'

'I can and I am,' Poole said snappily. 'Ladies, please get yourselves in the coach.'

Coral protested, 'I'm due to go on in Newburg tonight, *not* Stonewall.'

'And my ticket's to Newburg, too,' Jessica Dorne upheld.

They knew what was up. They'd heard Poole tell Will, and Poole knew it. That was why Chumser held a gun on them.

'Now, ladies,' Poole said, 'I've no wish to see harm

70

done to you, I really don't. But that Chinaman? Well, you've already seen he's different from us. Do you want me to spell it out for you?' he asked unpleasantly. Then he backed off, so that he could cover everyone. 'Get 'em in the coach.' he snapped.

It was Jessica Dorne that the Chinaman started for. She grabbed the greasy frying pan to defend herself, but Coral stepped in.

'I just love it honey, but it's no use,' she said. 'Put it down before they do us both some harm.' Then to Poole she said, 'I weren't *too* displeased with you, Mr Franklin Poole. But with you riskin' my career an' all . . . well now I'm kind o' hoping somebody catches up with you.'

'There's nothin' I did justifies that mob lynchin' me,' Poole answered back. Then he brandished the Colt. 'Will you now get aboard . . . *please?*'

Without further protest, both women made their way out to the coach. They looked totally exhausted, drained of the desire to fight back any more. The axe, sack of food supplies, the chain and wrist irons were carried out, and Will asked for Huck's watch.

Poole spoke to Pick Hammond. 'You've got enough food for a couple of days,' he said. 'By now, that Callister rider should be halfway to Newburg. They'll send out a posse an' I want you to tell 'em somethin'. Tell 'em, that if they follow me, if they start shootin' to try an' stop me from gettin' to Stonewall, a bullet's goin' to find one o' these lovely ladies.' Poole paused, stared hard at Hammond. 'You understand me, Deputy?' he demanded.

Hammond stared back at him, nodded once.

'Good, just make sure the posse understands then. The responsibility's all yours,' Poole told him.

They went to the coach and Will climbed up on to the driver's box, and unwound the reins from the brake handle. Poole settled beside him, and Chumser and the Chinaman sat back on the deck. Will took the stock of Huck's bull whip, cracked it out low and to the side of the team. Up and ahead of them, in the falling moonlight, they could see the darkness of the timberline, the distant peaks of the Sangre de Cristos.

12

Moonlight Ride

The first settlers into Horse Creek Territory had come over the old timber road when it was nothing more than an animal trace. Among them were Bewle Callister and Valentine Quirrel; the tough ex-army men looking for opportunity.

Blushing Lode was at the tail end of the Cristos on a low range called Broken Chimneys. For forty miles the old road went south, following the eastern flanks of the Chimneys down to the rim of the Pecos. There it met the road over which the Las Vegas–Santa Fe passenger and mail coaches passed. Then turning north for sixty miles was Stonewall and the Colorado border.

But now, in the moonlight, the Concord coach rolled through the soft runnels towards the town's abandoned mine shaft and the iron-rigged bridge that crossed the arroyo. Inside, the two women could see the massive bank of tailings, the gutted skeleton of the stamp-mill.

'I wonder what we're in for?' Coral said. 'Wonder if we'll *ever* get to see Newburg?'

'We will, but I'm not thinking that far ahead,' Jessica said. 'I'll let the Marshal do that.'

'Yeah, perhaps you're right. Funny ain't it – I've been most things, but never a hostage . . . not that I was aware of anyways. I'm just goin' to curl up on this seat . . . dream of bein' back in a good place.'

'But I do think that man Poole's bluffing,' Jessica added. 'Why would he harm us? It wouldn't help him any.'

'Well I wouldn't bet on that one, honey' Coral responded with a sigh. 'Let's just hope nobody calls his bluff. As it happens, I reckon he'll make it. So far he's turned bad into good.'

They were approaching the iron bridge now, and the roaring of the water got so loud, so incessant they stopped talking. But as they rumbled across the bridge, Jessica was still thinking about the undoubted spirit of Will Mitten.

They lost the moon behind the high Cristos, but they could still see the seething water as the road wound along the course of the widening arroyo. Countless storms and the passage of ore wagons had long since washed and worn the road to bedrock. In the climb to the mine shaft, the coach encountered little difficulty.

It wasn't long before the two women got drowsy from the ceaseless roar of the arroyo, and despite the often violent pitch of the coach they fell into an exhausted sleep. Jessica half woke once to hear voices as the men moved rock from where the road left the creek, then a little while later they both sat up as the moon appeared again. They passed the mine, saw its shaft and some caved-in roofs before they fell sleep again.

When they woke next, the coach had stopped and dawn was flowing orange and blue over the dark peaks of the Cristos. Coral and Jessica got out and stood uncertainly by the open door, watching Chumser trying to start a fire.

'There's a natural facility up beyond that pine, ladies. The water ain't too warm, but it's clean,' Poole called out while Chumser sniggered.

Chumser stood the coffee-pot on the fire as soon as the resin in the pine kindling flared. Poole and the Chinaman sat themselves on slabs of rock, Will on a log. No one spoke as the women emerged from the pine stand. The air was chilly, but the light was growing with the look of a bright, clear day.

'You ladies manage to get some sleep?' Poole asked, breaking the silence.

'I'm sure we've both had better nights,' Coral remarked sharply. 'Tell me, Poole, what are you going to do with us when we get to the border?' she asked.

'Well, I've been givin' it some thought. It'll be somethin' neither of you'll forget in a hurry – you can be sure o' that,' Poole said with a distinctive leer, and Chumser sniggered again.

'And if a posse catches up with us, you'll kill us?' Coral continued her questioning.

Poole almost laughed, shook his head. 'No lady, you're smart enough to know I wouldn't do that. What would be my gain?'

'Nothing. But maybe they'll know it too. What then?' Coral said.

'Well if they do start shootin' you both best duck. You wouldn't want to catch a stray bullet. It's simply a question of bluff.'

'You'll need more than a pair o' ladies to bluff those two old men.' Both Will and Coral smiled at her small joke.

'Maybe. But there'll be others who think twice about it. Others that'll be more circumspect with your lives, eh?' Poole suggested.

'They'll figure out a way to stop you, Frank. Even if they have to come at you alone,' Will joined in.

Poole shrugged. 'Hope they do. I'll finish the job off.' Then he turned to look at Chumser who was searching around the front boot of the coach. 'Get that keg over here,' he called, curiously in good humour.

They all had brandy in their coffee, even Jessica. As she sipped the hot fiery liquid, she shuddered. At her feet, a distressed lizard skittered across the loose shale, and downstream a blue heron flapped noisily from its roost. She looked around at the mariposa and ocotillo, flowers she'd only read about or seen in picture-books. 'Some other time, some other place,' she thought, almost bitterly.

'How long you figure it would take 'em to raise a posse, once that Callister rider got to Newburg?' she heard Poole ask Will.

'Two minutes. Out o' town in three if your name got mentioned,' Will told him without hesitation.

'Hmm, that long? Well, they ought to be ridin' into Blushin' Lode about now, then,' Poole said, getting to his feet. 'All aboard for Stonewall,' he told them. 'Let's roll some wheels.'

13

Rolling South

Will Mitten knew why Poole had halted the coach where he did, why he'd waited for the dawn, why he'd asked about the posse. Less than a mile beyond where they'd stopped, the timber road turned from the pine stands, ran clear along the eastern flank of the Chimneys. On a fine day you could see right to Newburg. So equally, the coach could be seen by riders heading towards Blushing Lode. If the posse saw the coach, they wouldn't ride into the Lode, they'd ride on, swing direct up the lower slopes. And in that case, Pick Hammond wouldn't be telling them about the women hostages.

Before they came out of the pine, Poole had Will stop the coach while he got down and walked ahead. He stared west, towards the distant Newburg, then he brought the coach on. There was thin early mist below them, which meant they could neither see nor be seen, meant the posse would have reached Blushing Lode. Right now, they'd probably be galloping hell-bent on the road behind them.

'What would you do if you were Quirrel or Callister?' Poole asked Will.

'If I was them,' Will repeated, 'as soon as I'd spoke to Hammond, I'd send a rider back to Newburg. Get a wire sent to US Marshals in Vegas *and* Santa Fe.' Will looked cannily at Poole. 'Callister, Quirrel, me . . . we'd both get *that* right. You can't just cross any old place with a Concord. Wherever we turn up, they'll be waitin'.'

Poole shook his head. 'But they'll respect hostage women,' he said.

'You're soundin' like a goddamn Comanche,' Will responded. 'They'll barricade the roads if we ever get that far.'

Poole laughed. 'There's wagon crossin's that nobody knows about, Will. From Raton to Durango, it's border trash country . . . riff-raff from the railroad camps. There's some call 'em "Reavers". They'll kill anythin', but it's mostly stock. They sell the hides a dollar apiece down in El Paso.'

Will listened attentively as Poole continued.

'I know that country. Holed up thereabouts for more'n a year when I ran from Eagle Spring. I can hide this coach from any posse. Take it on up to Arroyo Hondo on a trail you, nor anyone else, could find. We'll be halfway home, an' there'll be no US Marshals along either. They know to stay well away from them parts.'

'You're thinkin' too long-term, Frank,' Will said after a moment's thought. 'You'll never get beyond the Pecos.'

'Why, what's . . . *who's* to stop me?' Poole asked outwardly unruffled.

'For Chris'sakes there's *this* road . . . the one we're on. *This* is the one they'll block.'

'Pah, let 'em try,' said Poole. 'I've got six strong bays, tools an' rope. What can they build that I can't pull down?'

Nothing. But they could stand off, remain hidden, swat us like flies, Will thought.

Poole, as Will thought he would, said there'd be a change in the riding arrangements. Poole said he'd ride in the front cargo boot and the Chinaman and Chumser would either be in the rear boot or the passenger section. The ladies would also alternate, one up with Will, the other inside. They'd start off with the Chinaman in the rear boot, and Jessica Dorne on the driver's box.

The hinged covers of the boots were in two halves which could be swung up and out. They could be propped open, so that from the front boot, Poole could see above him and the road ahead, and speak to Will if he had a mind to. Within the relative safety of the boots, and in the passenger section, no one could be picked off by any lawful sharpshooter.

To put one of the women on the box would discourage any such attack and protect Will. But the marshal grimly reflected that the posse might figure he was travelling readily with his old friend Poole, and maybe have shares in the contents of Quirrel's iron-bound chest.

For a long time Jessica Dorne said nothing, but neither did Will. Then after nearly a half hour, when the horses had slowed to a walk around a tight bend in the road, she said quietly, 'I just saw someone, Marshal.'

'Where?' Will asked quick but casual. He wasn't surprised. Since they'd started off again, he'd sensed others on the mountain slopes. The country was too still. He'd seen a pair of buzzards rise, circle lazily in the thermals until whatever had disturbed them passed by. He'd hoped the birds were beyond the angle of Poole's view.

'Back to the left . . . our left,' Jessica said. 'Something moved . . . between two tree stumps. It was a man. Would it be them – the posse following?' she asked.

Will nodded. 'Could be. Can't think who else would be up here.'

'What do you think they'll do?'

Will shook his head. He wanted to keep their voices down below the sound of the horses and the creak and groan of the coach. 'If the time comes when there's shootin',' he whispered hoarsely, 'get down and lie flat.'

The quiet descended again as they rode, each with their own troubled thoughts.

It was another half hour that passed before Jessica spoke. 'I'm sorry Marshal,' she started, 'but I don't normally have anything important or interesting to say . . . or so I'm told.' She watched, waited for his reaction.

'You just talk, I'll decide,' he said. 'I'll wager you're interestin' enough to keep me awake.' Without saying so, Will was feeling the pressure of his toil, the distress of responsibility and no sleep.

Jessica decided to ask a question. 'Why was it named Blushing Lode?' she asked.

'What?' he asked, confused.

'Blushing Lode. Why's it so called?'

'Oh, yeah. Well, there's minerals along the arroyo,' he said. 'Mainly copper . . . some zinc an' stuff. Now an' again, when the water's high it picks up colour. An' when the sun catches it, it turns red, looks like it's . . . well you can imagine.'

'Yes. That's a nice way to get named. How about Eagle Spring?'

'Comanches used to lie in wait for fish eagles in Horse Creek. Catchers, they called 'em. They'd hide under the cut banks . . . wait for one to swoop down for a steelhead lure. Then they'd spring out an' seize their legs. It was the big, barred wing feathers they wanted – stuck'em in their hair. "Countin' coup", they called it. A rite of manhood.'

Jessica gave a small, impressed smile. 'Well that's the places I've *been*,' she said. 'Tell me about Newburg. It doesn't sound quite so . . . so. . . .' She went quiet, and could see that Will was distracted.

The marshal was looking back to where Jessica had indicated movement in the trees. But there was noth-

82

ing to see, and Will was guessing that if it had been a member of the posse, by now they'd have figured out what to do next.

For a while Jessica thought about what Will had been telling her. 'I don't *really* want to know about Newburg.' she said. 'That's for another time. After last night, I realize how important today is. Life's been so safe for me, Marshal.'

'Yes ma'am, I can well imagine, even though "safe's" not a word I'd associate with Eagle Spring.'

Jessica was going to say something else, but saw that Will's interest had changed again. He was looking at fresh tracks in the road ahead, and knew that Poole in the boot must be able to see them too. The tracks angled off the road along a trail that led up over a broken ridge. Where they hit the road, he reined in the team.

'Looks like them "Reavers" we been told about,' he said loud enough for Poole to hear. He could see the prints of the unshod mules and horses, nine or ten strong.

Poole was looking up at the ridge. 'Yeah, reckon,' he agreed. 'Looks like they're on their way to them hot springs at Almeda.'

'Well it probably won't be to take a bath. We can just hope they keep on goin',' Will said grimly.

He released the brake, then moved the team off. Now he was exhausted and very troubled. As the day began to cool and shadows lengthened, he knew what those two revengeful old men would think, what they'd do when they cut the fresh tracks.

He knew that if the posse couldn't be persuaded to attack the coach, the border trash could be.

14

Peace Talks

Before full dark they hauled over for the night. Poole knew the place, choosing it from his memory of the road that he'd ridden over recently. Together with the Chinaman and Charlie Chumser, he'd camped in the same spot on their way up to Eagle Spring. The road doubled around a swathe of mountain grass that held a trout brook. There was a sheltering clump of jack-pine and an overhang of rock beside the road. On the far side, the grass ran out to a brink where the mountain suddenly ended.

They unhitched, and left the coach standing in the bend of the road where they'd build their fire. When they'd watered and fed the horses, they picketed them on the grass between the precipice and the coach. The moon would rise early, and a lookout lying atop behind the coach would see anyone coming along the road.

As soon as he'd finished with the horses, and been into the timber with a gun on him, they chained Will to a tree near to where Chumser was building the fire. The fatigued marshal had the dubious advantage of being the loser, and quickly went to sleep. The Chinaman, who would have the middle watch that night, also slept. Among them all, only the wounded Poole appeared lively.

As the fugitive sat sipping his brandy, staring into the fire, Coral watched him. She knew enough of him now to know how his mind would be working. He'd be looking ahead, trying to foresee every obstacle. He'd be wondering how to outwit and outrun those who were watching the glow of their fire from somewhere on the dark mountain.

For herself, she was wondering if those in the posse believed Poole would shoot her and Jessica if his getaway was endangered. She knew he'd be thinking about that. Like Will, she thought it would be so simple for them if they just shot the team first thing in the morning. Poole glanced up, saw her watching him. He smiled openly, and didn't look as if there was trouble to deal with.

'How far is it to the border?' she asked him.

'To Stonewall? At least another day . . . maybe two. Depends on how our friends out there decide to play their hand. Join me in a nightcap, why don't you, Miss Coral?'

'Don't mind if I do,' she said. Coral got up and walked over to the keg. 'And a drop more for you,' she suggested.

She glanced towards Jessica as she took Poole's drinking cup, seeing that except for Chumser on watch, Poole and herself were the only ones still awake. She poured the El Paso brandy and sat down near him. For a while they gazed silently into the darkness, then she said quietly, 'Who were those horsemen?'

'What horsemen?' he asked.

'The marshal saw their tracks; so did you.'

'They looked like rawhiders ... bad men, Miss Coral.'

'They ornery?'

'Well, there ain't much they like, save drink an' women,' he said, looking at her slyly.

'That's why you want to stay clear of 'em?' she wondered aloud.

'Yeah, that's exactly why,' Poole answered truthfully.

They were silent a moment, sipping their brandy. Finally, Coral said, 'If I'd got to Newburg, I'd be getting ready to do a number about now.'

Poole laughed softly. 'Just pretend you're there. Close your eyes ... do it in your head.'

For a moment they looked at each other, both trying to imagine the moment.

'No, it ain't workin'. All I can hear is that Chinaman snorin',' Coral said, and they both laughed.

'How's your shoulder? she asked.

'Like your singin'. I try an' imagine it's all right, but it ain't. Just carries on hurtin'. That's why I been tryin' to empty that keg.' He glanced up at the coach top. 'Charlie?' he called softly.

'Yeah?' Chumser answered.

'Nothin'. Just stay awake,' Poole warned him.

'When was that bandage put on?' Coral asked.

He thought a moment. 'Err, night before last. It's meant to be a sling.'

'Then it should be changed,' she said and stood up. 'I can help. I once saw my pa havin' a gunshot wound mended.'

'Well that's reassuring, but this ain't a gunshot wound, Miss. I got hit with a telegraph pole. Seems my luck's changed though. I been surrounded by medical experts ever since we left Eagle Spring,' he said, deeply cynical.

She put water on the fire to heat, then untied the sling and pulled Poole's shirt and undershirt carefully from his shoulder. She winced, seeing where the flesh of his upper arm and side had been beaten. It was dark, deeply bruised and spread wide.

'I can clean it up. A new dressing will make it feel better,' she said reassuringly.

'Why'd you want to do this?' Poole asked her as she began to bathe his sore skin.

'I'd do it for anybody . . . well *almost* anybody,' she said.

'Hmm. Not for somebody you wanted dead, then?'

'I guess not.'

'Then we can wrap this up. You're thinkin' . . . were hopin' that if everythin' was. . . ?'

'You got something to say, Mr Poole?'

'Yeah. It know it don't seem the thing, but maybe you want me to stick around?'

Her eyes met his and held a moment, the night veiled her colour. 'Yeah, maybe.' she said.

15

The Sheriff's Bid

Up on a ridge, a mile back from the coach, another small fire of pine wood flared into the night. It silhouetted the two men who sat beside it, casting yellow highlights on the bits of the two saddled horses that stood near.

In the firelight, Pick Hammond's stubbled face looked haggard. The other man, who was another of Bewle Callister's riders, could see the dark swollen forehead where the Chinaman had felled Hammond the night before. Rud Northwick ran his tongue along the paper of the cigarette he was building.

'Shouldn't think you'd be treadin' too softly – not after what they done to you,' he said. 'I'd want blood an' bodies if that was *my* head.'

Hammond stared long-sufferingly at him. 'Yeah, but unfortunately I'm a lawman, so this ain't personal. You Callister hands don't seem to cotton on to that, do you?'

'What do you mean?'

'I know what him and Quirrel are up to,' Hammond said.

'What's that?'

'They've bought you an' your support. Probably told you those women on the coach are hookers. Told you to forget 'em . . . leave 'em to the wolves. You're just to get the gold back, an' Frank Poole o' course.'

Callister's man shook his head slowly. 'Poole's playin' pretend. He ain't goin' to shoot anyone with us on his tail.'

'No?' Hammond said. 'What's he got to lose? And that goddamn John China would slit his own Granma's throat. He'd do it for the hell of it . . . or whatever he believes in.'

'Well, I figure them women just got to take their chances,' Northwick said.

'*Callister* does your figurin', Northwick. You ain't got the wits to do anythin' else. You make me sick.'

Northwick stared at him. 'But you're the one won't have a job left when you get back to Eagle Spring. *If* you ever get back,' he ventured.

'Yes,' Hammond said, but that was all. They'd both heard the sound of a horse approaching. Then a voice spoke out of the darkness.

'Hold your fire, I'm comin' in.'

Hammond immediately recognized Morgan Kinney as the rider. He got to his feet. 'Marshal, it's me, Pick' he called. 'Ride in.'

There were small snuffles and harness chinks as Kinney rode into the marginal light of the fire. He dismounted and came to the fire and tossed down his saddle-bags. For a moment he stood looking at his deputy.

'They got the telegraph fixed then?' Hammond acknowledged.

'Yeah,' Kinney said. 'Early this mornin'. I heard from Newburg about noon. Callister's posse sent a rider back as soon as they got the story from the Lode. I set right out.' He glanced around him as he spoke. 'Where are they? Is Quirrel here?'

Hammond pushed the coffee jug back into the embers. 'Yeah, him an' Callister. They rode to the Almeda springs. Went before dark to parley with some rawhiders whose trail we crossed.'

'They ain't rawhiders. They're Reavers – scum you don't normally grace with a name.' Kinney spat his words contemptuously. 'An' you don't need a trail to know they're around. You can smell 'em from ten mile, an' I'd like to know what those old curs want with 'em?' He hunkered down, held his hands out to the fire.

Hammond kneeled beside him. 'What did you hear from Newburg?' he asked.

'The lot, I guess . . . up to the coach pullin' out o' the Lode,' Kinney said. He looked sharply at his deputy. 'You an' Will Mitten sure must have been desperate to turn them prisoners loose at the bridge?'

92

'Yeah, you had to have been there. It was get 'em to help, or drown. Turned out wrong, but I reckon we done the right thing,' Hammond told him. 'But now the coach is up here, pulled off the old road. The team are picketed close by with Jale Stetter's horse.'

'Who killed Stetter?' Kinney asked.

'The Chinaman,' said Hammond. 'They're well hid an' Poole don't show himself. If we did put a bullet in him, I figure the heathen'd kill one o' the women for the fun of it and take Stetter's mount.'

'Yeah. But what's to stop Poole doin' that when the light goes?' Kinney understandably asked.

'There's men posted along the road above and behind the coach, an' he probably knows it. Anyhow, the last thing he wants to do is leave the coach.'

Kinney shook his head. 'He'll never get that gold into Colorado.'

'Well he sure as hell aims to take a crack at it – that's for sure.'

'What are Quirrel an' Callister up to?'

'They're goin' to try an' get them rawhiders – Comancheros – whatever they are, to attack the coach.'

Kinney looked distressed at the news. 'Yeah,' he said, 'that makes sense. They'll have some cruel amusement. Do things a posse'd never get blamed for.'

Hammond screwed his face up, blinked hard at the thought of what that meant.

'Poole's no heifer brain. He'll know what's up.'

'I know ... told 'em so. But I was outvoted,' Hammond said. As he poured them hot coffee, Northwick suddenly got up.

'It's them,' he said.

While the posse rode into camp and dismounted, Kinney quietly sipped his coffee. 'It ain't a matter of votin', he declared sternly.

Morgan Kinney sat unmoved as Callister and Quirrel came over to face him across the fire. They were men who never went without, and brought along a pack horse laden with fresh meat, beans and bread. Some of the men started to cut frying steaks, another got more coffee on the go and bottles of whiskey and beer were passed around. In spite of their power and wealth, Quirrel and Callister were dressed beaver. But they had big guns buckled around their coats, and carried hard unforgiving looks. Among the bunch, Kinney noticed Lane Manners, his official counterpart of Newburg, talking to Northwick.

When Kinney had drained his coffee he spoke to them. 'I hear you're gettin' some rabble from the border to attack the coach,' he stated.

Quirrel blinked, staring as if he'd just noticed Kinney sitting there. 'You got a better idea?' he demanded.

Kinney stood up slowly and faced him. 'Oh, I got a better idea, but I asked you the question. Remember I'm a law officer.'

'That's in Eagle Spring. Up here you ain't got more'n spit,' Quirrel interrupted gruffly.

94

'I'm accountable to the US Marshal. That's Will Mitten,' Kinney said. 'In his absence, *I'm* the Federal officer along the Horse Creek . . . not Lane Manners. Now, bearin' that in mind, it seems to me you could be in Federal trouble . . . incitement trouble.'

'You accountable to Poole too?' Callister rasped at him.

Kinney caught the watery sheen of the old man's pale eyes. 'I'll ignore that, on account of you bein' just a whoop an' a holler from pasture,' he said after a long moment.

Then Callister made a suggestion. 'You think Will Mitten ain't in cahoots with his old pal, eh Sheriff?'

'That's rubbish, an' you know it,' Kinney snapped back at him. 'Anyone who knows Will would know that.'

'It's what *I* think, an' *I* know him.' Callister said smugly.

'A marshal's badge ain't worth more than fifty thousand dollars. That's the worth o' my gold dust,' Quirrel sniped at Kinney.

'Yeah, a lot more, but it wouldn't buy Will Mitten,' Kinney returned quickly.

'Would you have been dumb enough to release those prisoners to fill a hole in the ground?' Callister kept up with the tirade.

'I can't say. Perhaps if I'd been there . . . who knows? Will was thinkin' of more than himself,' Kinney said. 'A strange notion for you to take in, Mr Callister.'

'I'd think the thousand-dollar reward for Poole's capture wouldn't make you too particular about the health of him or anyone else on that coach,' Quirrel said.

Kinney swore. 'There's something repellent about you, Quirrel. Rich, but still sickening. An' the money goes to Jabber Nibbs's widow,' he added with bile.

Quirrel looked at Callister, and they both shook their heads as if they didn't understand or care.

Kinney turned to his deputy. 'What exactly did Poole say to you about the women, Pick?' he asked him.

'He told me they'd send out a posse. I had to tell 'em that if they followed, if they started shootin' or tried to stop him from gettin' to Stonewall, he'd shoot 'em. Then he asked me if I understood . . . told me to make sure *they* did. He said the responsibility was mine.'

Callister spat into the ground around his feet. 'Alley cats,' he said.

'It wouldn't make any difference if they were,' Kinney said, 'but they ain't. One of 'em's not much more'n a kid. Now I'll ask you again about that border rabble you been dealin' with.'

'Rabble? What's this rabble you keep on about, Sheriff?' Callister snarled. He glanced around him. 'You men know about any *rabble?*'

But there was no response, except some of the men shook their heads, turned away sheepishly. Kinney sucked at a tooth, noticed that Manners had moved out of his line of sight.

'Listen, Kinney!' Quirrel shouted. 'Franklin Poole killed my son. You understand that? Now you're doin' your damnedest to protect him,' he charged the sheriff from Eagle Spring.

'We're goin' to catch that killer, with or without

your help, Kinney,' Callister said hostilely. He took an aggresive step towards the sheriff. 'I been seekin' his blood since the day he shot my boy. Louis was all I had, an' the law ain't havin' Poole, just to let him go again.' He advanced another pace on Kinney, shook a hard old fist. 'You can have his bones when I'm finished with him – there'll be no meat left on 'em.'

Kinney understood the situation and took a few deep breaths, then waited while the wrath of the two men settled down. Then he turned to face them, and the riders who'd rode in with them.

'You're prepared to sacrificed the lives of two girls for Frank Poole,' he said, not expecting an answer. The town sheriff of Newburg had taken up his place behind Quirrel, and Kinney saw him. Like the town itself, Lane Manners was another of Quirrel's properties.

'Did you deputize everybody in this posse, Brett?' Kinney asked him.

Manners nodded. 'Yep, everybody,' he said.

'Well no crime was committed at Newburg. You got less jurisdiction than me, an' I ain't leadin' a mob . . . a lynchin' party. But right now I'm goin' to let it pass, you takin' the law into your own hands . . . Quirrel's hands. But I ain't goin' to forget it.'

He paused, stared for a moment into the faces of Quirrel and Callister. 'As long as we're in Horse Creek Territory, I'm takin' charge of this posse.'

As he said it, the two old men growled scornfully and met each other's eyes. 'Get us some coffee, Lane,' Quirrel said rudely.

Exasperated and angered, Kinney watched Manners pour the men's coffee, then he spoke up again. 'Poole's warned us that he'll kill the women if we so much as bother him,' he said.

'He's bluffin',' Callister rumbled.

Kinney smashed a fist into the palm of one hand. 'You reckon he's bluffin', eh? Well let me tell you this. If one of them women's harmed, a single hair o' their head, as a result of an attack by, or on behalf of this posse, I'll have you all charged with attempted murder.'

Kinney waited, let his words sink home, watching each man's face. He knew that the posse were suckies, apple-polishers to Quarrel and Callister, but he hoped that a few would stand with him if he told them the truth, the price they'd be paying.

'What you want us to do, Kinney? Give 'em an escort to Colorado?' Callister sneered.

'No,' Kinney said. 'We'll ride along . . . watch and wait. There'll be a time.'

Callister continued. 'Don't know what you mean by "on behalf of". You been told, we know nothin' about any goddamn border rabble.'

Kinney just stared. He knew it didn't matter any more. It was too late to do anything about it. As far as Quirrel and Callister were concerned, his words didn't amount to a hill of beans. Quirrel and Callister weren't fearful of any gods or devils, let alone a sheriff's badge and a Federal authority.

16

Rockslide

Franklin Poole took early-morning watch on the coach deck. The Chinaman woke him about two o'clock. Will was awake too. He was sitting in the moonlight in his chains, pondering, watching the food that had been left for him.

'We're likely to get hit just before first light,' Poole said in a low voice. 'You know that, Will?'

'Yeah, I know it. You better let me have the carbine.'

Poole laughed. 'I got me a woman who can shoot guns,' he said. 'An' I got China an' Charlie, too. What more could a man want?'

'They'll wait for the moon to drop. They won't have long, but you won't see 'em.'

'Let's hope they don't see us, then,' Poole said. 'We'll tie the horses into the trees.'

*

Just before the moon disappeared behind the peaks of the Chimneys, when Huck Ambler's stem-winder said five o'clock, Poole woke the Chinaman and Charlie Chumser. One by one, they led the horses from their patch of mountain grass and tied them into the clump of jack-pine that screened their camp from the ridge. Then they unchained Will from his tree, took him at gunpoint to the coach, and chained him in there with Jessica Dorne.

Poole tossed aside his makeshift sling and got up on the deck behind a couple of feed bags. He handed Coral the carbine, posted Chumsser and the Chinaman in the pine. Then they waited, watching the moon slip behind the mountains.

When the Reavers came, they came from two directions. One group picked its way down from the ridge, another group came up the road from the south.

From the coach deck, Poole and Coral could see those coming along the road. They were silhouetted against the dark, clear-bright sky and Poole took the carbine back from Coral. It was awkward, painful, but he aimed low and fired, then levered in another shell before the approaching riders loosed off their hostile guns.

The three men immediately pulled their horses away and ran from the road. They made it to the patch of mountain grass where the coach team had been picketed, circled with their accomplices down from the ridge. They yelled chilling, enraged threats, galloped noisily past the coach as the Chinaman and Chumser opened up from the trees. In the coach, Jessica impulsively clung to Will Mitten, but he held her down against the seat as some of the bullets from Chumser's wild shooting tore through the side panels of the coach. Then abruptly, the night-shattering noises stopped. The attackers regrouped, fired off another withering hail of lead, then whirled away, riding fast on to the road ahead.

Within seconds the mountain was again swathed in its habitual quiet. But Poole wasted no time. China and Chumser ran from the trees, guarded Will as he calmed the horses and hurriedly made the hitch. Poole walked into the middle of the road, arrogantly looked around, then swept his eyes along the dark crest of the ridge, back along the road.

'Next attack, an' a girl dies. You hear me?' he yelled, the echo reverberating up into the mountain slopes.

Deeply troubled now, Will doubled up on his cursing. He knew that any move the Newburg posse made, any move that might lead to recapture, or even killing of his former prisoners, the women would be in danger. He also knew that if he managed to get the coach into its final run north, the presence of the women wouldn't stop Callister and Quirrel, not with the border less than a day away.

As light stretched in from the east, Poole gave Jessica a hand down from the coach. He walked her forward, and as the sun rose over the distant Horse Creek he let her go, watching as she stood defenceless and alone in the middle of the road. For anyone watching it was a tragic but shrewd reminder about the risk they'd be taking if they attacked again.

The coach rolled further south, along the old timber road. The horses were fed and watered, arguably rested, and when they wanted to run, Will gave them their head. The others were riding as before: the Chinaman in the rear boot and Coral up on the box. Poole was in the front boot again, Jessica and Chumser inside.

The day broke warm and clear. The mountains were now getting behind them, snowy peaks thrusting into the mighty New Mexican sky. Had he not known better, Will would have said they travelled safe and alone. The road was good, for long stretches offered no obstacles. Once a fallen knobcone pine stopped them and Will had to unhitch the team. They hauled the big timber aside, used the break to eat some bacon and biscuit, but were soon on their way again. As the day wore on, Poole began to talk to Will.

'We could be in Stonewall day after tomorrow,' he said. Then after a moment's silence, 'You ever been to Colorado, Will?'

'No, never quite made it.'

'There's enough gold here under my feet for both of us,' Poole said. 'You'd like Colorado, Will. It's real law-abidin' too. Wouldn't need to go around breakin' it. We could buy land – more than Bewle Calliser ever dreamed of.'

'I don't want more land than Bewle Callister. All I

want is more land than I got at the moment, so that ain't much of an issue.'

Will had been sure that Poole would come on to him sometime. In a way he'd dreaded it; forced to hold the pompous disinterest, the slur on his lawful ways. But his reputation would be ruined along Horse Creek. If Poole escaped, he'd be branded guilty of having made the escape possible for his old friend. Ironically, and to Poole's way of thinking, entirely possible that he could be persuaded. If he agreed to Poole's proposition, he knew he'd be unchained, even given back his gun.

Will had thought it through that morning before the attack. He knew that if the road broke up and the coach couldn't go on. the situation would worsen for Coral and Jessica. He'd be left behind and so would Quirrel's iron-bound chest. Poole would have to run off though, and use the girls as a safeguard against the posse's bullets. Then there'd be improved dead-or-alive rewards from Callister and Quirrel for Poole. But Will knew that as long as there were rapacious, reckless men in the posse, they'd construe *that* as meaning *dead.*

For a while he'd wriggled on the horns of his dilemma. Then, life being what it is, he made up his mind: Jessica Dorne's security was more important than his word. And with a gun, he might even make a fighting comeback.

'What you got to lose?' Poole asked him, as if he fully understood. 'What you goin' to do . . . besides look for another job?'

Will felt a nerve twitch in his jaw. Jessica was look-ing at him and he looked to see if he could estimate her thoughts.

'Think to get a job clerkin' in a store'? My old man did that. You remember, Will?' Poole went on. 'No, you're goin' to have to throw in with me. There's nothin' much else, unless you turn to preachin' about salvation, eh Will?'

Will drew a deep breath. 'Supposin' . . . just supposin' I give it a thought?' he asked. 'What happens?'

'Together we get this coach across the border. I've got friends up in Stonewall,' Poole said, getting hopeful. 'We'll blow the box, an' I'll pay the boys out o' my half share. Just think, Will – twenty-five thou-sand dollars . . . *each*.'

Quirrel's gold was more than twenty years of a sheriff's pay. Will tried to say he'd think it over, but he couldn't. He could feel it, suffer it, just couldn't say it. And after the look he saw on Jessica Dorne's face, it was obvious she knew it too.

Throughout the long day they saw nothing: no smoke, no tracks. In the afternoon, they'd made good time; nearly as much as they'd made in the morning. When the first shadows moved into the mountain and first dark approached, they stopped fifty yards from the mouth of a gully. For long moment, no one made a sound. They were almost cowed by the depth of silence, no sounds of hoofs and harness, the never-ending chew of wheels over

104

the hard packed flinty ground.

But Will Mitten was staring at a rockslide, and knew they'd be going no further that day, if they did ever. An outcrop had fallen on to the road, and all they could see ahead of them was a steeply rising pile of loose rock.

Poole had Jessica get down, walk with him and Will to the tail of the slide.

'It's still warm,' Poole said drily. Then he peered at the ledges and ridges above. 'What's the bettin' we'll find boot tracks up there?' he said. He turned to Will. 'How long you figure it's going to hold us up?'

Will pushed back his hat. 'I'd say 'til kingdom come. We ain't ever goin' to shift all this, Frank. I'd like to see what's it's like on the other side,' he said.

Chumser had got out of the coach with Jessica and the Chinaman, and Poole called him forward.

'You get on up there, Charlie,' he told him. 'Tell us what you see.'

Chumser took a long considerate look at the talus, kneeling to remove the boots he'd taken off Lovecraft. Then on all fours, he climbed in his sockless feet. When he got to the top he looked ahead, and called back to Poole.

'Looks the same this side.'

'How's the road up ahead?' Poole shouted at him.

'There's a bend. Give me a minute, I'll go see.'

After the initial sound of Chumser's descent on the other side of the slide, silence descended again. They waited and Will felt the dread, the certainty of their mistake.

105

Poole felt it too. 'Chumser . . . Charlie!' he yelled.

The name bounced eerily off the gully walls, and nearby a lone poorwill squawked. Somewhere a loose rock chinked and scuffled, and that was it.

'Charlie,' Poole called again, and again the name echoed, fell away to nothing.

After a long, charged few seconds, Poole turned to Will. 'We got to know. You go ahead of me,' he said firmly. 'You get between us, but stay down at the top,' he told Coral. 'Stay here,' he ordered the Chinaman.

Resigned to his fate, and Poole's gun. Will picked his way over the loose rock and started up the slide. As he neared the top he crawled low, waited for a while then lifted his head.

Chumser was a short distance ahead of the slide. He was lying near the edge of the road, close to a sharp bend. He was spread-eagled in the dust, his face staring into the sun. His neck was a bloody gash, and the ground around his head was turning dark.

Will swore vehemently. He twisted around, called out to Poole. 'You sent him to his death, Frank. He's lyin' here with his head half cut off.'

Poole stumbled on up the slide. He stared at Chumser and Will saw him swallowing hard. For a moment, the two men faced the land ahead of them. Beyond the stony debris, the sides of the gully rose up. The bend in the road was partly screened by agave and scrub pine.

'Quirrel an' Callister paid them goddamn Reavers to do that,' Poole quietly rasped.

'That's one way o' lookin' at it, Frank. Some folk'd

106

say Charlie's blood's on your hands.' The disgust was evident in Will's voice.

'Will you go get him, if I cover you?' Poole asked.

'Yeah, I'll go.' Will stood up slowly. He scanned the scrubby vegetation, then made his way down to the road. He walked unwaveringly forward, staring down at Chumser's dirty, bare feet. He waved the tip of his boot at the blow-flies that had already found the warm, gaping flesh beneath Chumser's open mouth.

Will part-carried, part-dragged the body back up over the slide. Poole was taking a step away when Jessica Dorne's startled scream rived the mountain-side. Will let go of Chumser's ankle, and looked up to see her struggling with the Chinaman near the coach. When Poole yelled he instinctively saw his chance. But he didn't have time. As he made a move, Poole turned back, and he was staring into the muzzle of his own Colt.

But the Chinaman had released Jessica. Her eyes were blazing, and she slapped him hard around his face as she pulled herself away.

'Get your hands off her,' Coral cried, running away from the slide towards them.

Will had caught hold of Chumser again. He lugged him to the side of the coach, laid him down.

Poole said to the Chinaman in a blunt, wounding voice. 'Touch her again, and I'll kill you.' Then he turned to Will. 'You gettin' ready to jump me back there?'

'I wanted my gun back.'

'Yeah, I can guess what for,' Poole said appreciatively. Then he nodded sternly at the rockslide. 'We'll make a ramp – haul the coach up an' over. How long's it goin' to take to fix this side?' he asked.

'For a ramp to take a Concord? Three, maybe four hours.'

'The other side?'

'We'll get down there OK. Goin' up's the problem.'

'Better get started then. You're movin' rock,' Poole said grimly.

Will looked with incredulity as his one-time friend persisted.

'They won't stop me, Will. Not you or anybody's goin' to do that.'

17

Keeping Watch

On the old timber road, where the eastern bulwarks of Broken Chimneys ran down to the rim of the Pecos, the main body of the posse had also come to a halt. A smokeless, greasewood fire was burning and coffee was going. When the horses were cared for, the men sat around the fire and passed around the bottles.

That morning after he'd gone down and studied the scene of the raid, Kinney realized that the two men who'd been sent to nightwatch the road hadn't returned to camp. He also knew that Bewle Callister's rider, Rud Northwick, was missing, and he'd had to guess at why. Consequently, he'd sent Pick Hammond riding ahead, while the main body of the posse kept pace with the coach. Although he'd told them all of his authority, he'd known it was a pale, ineffective statement. Out there on the rim of the

109

Pecos, he led no one other than his deputy.

Quirrel and Callister had cut him out. All day he'd watched the two of them making their way through the posse, talking confidential and snide as they rode. He knew what they were doing though: upping the bounty on Franklin Poole.

As the afternoon waned they'd met up with Northwick and the two other riders. They were cold-harboured alongside one of the many fast-running mountain brooks. Their horses were grazing and the two riders were sprawled out asleep. Northwick had his hand trailing in the water tickling for trout.

'Where's my deputy . . . Pick Hammond?' Kinney asked.

Northwick jerked his head to the south. 'Down there, I reckon.' He didn't look at Kinney, just at Callister and Quirrel. The two old men were sitting their horses like warring generals.

'Here tell, there's a big son-of-a-bitch rockslide down on the timber road,' he said casually.

Kinney cursed and swung his horse, then dug spurs. For nearly an hour he followed tracks south. He rode through high country until the land broke and he came across Hammond's chestnut mare tied in to a stand of young alders. He dismounted, tied his own horse, and pulled a telescope from his saddle-bags.

He knew Hammond would be thinking evidence, and would have rode off to see if Northwick and his cohorts were involved in the rockslide. Avoiding a clear viewpoint along the road, he cautiously

110

emerged from the pines. He followed horse and boot tracks along the timber-pocketed slope until he heard the coach on the road below. He stopped, listened to the rolling crunch of the iron-treaded wheels, the clatter of hoofs on scree. Then he saw his deputy coming towards him.

'That vermin Northwick said there's been a rock-slide,' Kinney alleged without preamble.

'Yeah. But you can't see too good from up here – it's the mouth of a gully,' Hammond replied. 'I was about to ride on some . . . find a better vantage. I'd seen enough here . . . heard you comin'.'

'It was Northwick started it?'

Hammond nodded. 'Got to be. About an hour after I left the posse behind, I heard this noise. I thought it was trees fallin'. With the storm, the streams cuttin' the earth from the roots. But I reckon it was the rockslide. You know what. . . ?'

'Yeah, I know, Pick,' Kinney said, holding up his hand for silence.

As Hammond stopped talking, Kinney listened. He couldn't hear the sound of the coach any longer. 'Any sign they started that slide?' he asked. He didn't doubt it, or his deputy. He was just thinking through the evidence, his testimony.

'Proofs difficult. But there's sign,' Hammond said. 'An' there's tracks.'

'What's the sign?'

'I found some big pine stakes. You can see they used 'em as pries to shift the rock. The slide's fresh as well – dust's hardly settled.'

111

Kinney nodded, and thought for a moment before he spoke. 'I want to see. Let's get down there . . . get us a good look. If that fall's goin' to hold up the coach, there'll be a turkey shoot round here.'

'How's things with the posse?' Hammond asked.

Kinney shrugged. 'I've got no control over 'em. Might as well bark at knots. I can't ride after every man that rides off, order him back with a gun at his head. An' I cant keep Quirrel and Callister from uppin' the odds . . . offerin' more bounty.'

'Anybody we can count on?'

'A few maybe,' Kinney said as they started back towards their mounts. 'There's Monk Pawley, he's Lane Manners' new deputy over there at Newburg. The two new young riders for Callister seem OK – Marden and Darnley Finnis, I think they're called. At least they look me in the eye when I say somethin'. Most o' the others are just bad guys.'

The law men mounted, then rode through a downward spine of rock to where Hammond had indicated a more useful standpoint. When they were about halfway they reined in sharply. Through the timber, they'd both seen two of the hostile and fearful Reavers. Both were riding tough, brush mounts, carried Sharps rifles slung across their backs, and had foot-long Bowie knives hanging low at their hips. They'd walked up the spine, and faded almost instantly into the thickening knobcone along the crest of the ridge.

'What the hell do you reckon they're doin' here?' Kinney asked.

'Huntin'. They got to eat . . . same as us regular folk.' But Hammond knew that couldn't be right. The sound of a gunshot would carry for miles and wasn't a Reavers way.

Ten minutes later they saw where the men had hobble-hitched their horses. They dismounted, tied in their own close by. Then they crawled forward on their bellies, through the scrub to where they could look down into the gully, see the rockpile on the old timber road.

'Whew, but I bet it don't stop 'em for more'n a few hours,' Kinney said, sounding curiously pleased. It was at that moment that they heard Jessica Dorne's yell. Kinney's jaw dropped, then he snapped open his spyglass. Hammond saw his neck and jaw muscles tighten as he studied the pile of rock.

'Jeeesus,' Kinney said, and passed the spyglass to his deputy. 'What do you make o' that,' he asked quietly.

'Unless Poole's been takin' a piss, there's a pool o' somethin' real nasty this side o' the pile,' Hammond answered after a few seconds. 'Where the hell's them Reavers, Morg?'

'They *were* down there. Somebody from the coach must have come over the top of the slide to have a look at the road. They were waitin'.'

Beyond that Kinney didn't know. But he speculated on whether it was something to do with the girl's scream. The blood-stained dirt wasn't from a flesh wound and he hoped it wasn't Will Mittens.

He knew the first thing Callister and Quirrel

would have done after he'd rode off was send one or two riders to catch him. And he knew they'd skin Rud Northwick for giving slack to Hammond.

The marshal from Newburg rolled on to his back. He closed his eyes for a few seconds, wondering what Will Mitten was doing.

He left Hammond with the spyglass, rode out to meet Callister's riders. There were three of them, and he told them where to find Hammond. He reminded them that unless they wanted to face charges later, they were being led by a deputy sheriff, and advised them not to do anything Pick Hammond didn't tell them to.

But as he rode back to the posse, he knew his words meant little to the stern men. They'd nodded agreeably, but hadn't met his eyes.

18

The Prospects

By the time Morgan Kinney got back to the posse's camp, first dark and cold breezes were pressing through the trees.

Bewle Callister and Valentine Quirrel, wrapped in warm Ganado rugs, sat with their stiff backs against a pine. In the firelight their hard-set features looked deathlike, and made Kinney shudder. Self-importantly they turned their faces towards him as he closed on the fire.

'They're already startin' to get the rock moved,' he said provokingly. He stared at their faces, wanting a reaction. 'One of 'em's been killed. Look's like a knifin'. That'll be the work o' that murderin' scum you been payin'. So I tell you this: when that rock-slide you two paid for's moved, there'll be retaliation.' Kinney met the glassy, unblinking stares of the two oldsters, then continued.

'If it's Mitten they killed, I'll see both your scrawny necks stretched in Fort Scott. An' if it weren't Poole, you've left him no other choice. He'll be playin' for his life now, an' knows it. And don't forget that if Mitten is alive, you got to concede his lawful authority . . . 'cause he's *still* a US Marshal.'

Valentine Quirrel glanced at Callister. 'Whatever's happened ain't to do with us, Kinney. What you got other than notions?' he challenged.

'None of it's goin' to stand up in court, I'll grant you.' Kinney replied. 'But now every man here knows that blood's on your hands. Poole and Mitten will know it too an' them girls, whose lives you so readily threaten.'

Bewle Callister spoke up. 'Listen, Mister,' he snarled. 'You had your say last night. Told us how Poole would figure we set Reavers on 'em, how he'd kill one of them women to spite. Well, Mister, he didn't, 'cause he's bluffin'.'

'Yeah, so you keep sayin', Callister. But that don't mean much,' Kinney snapped back. 'He warned you . . . an' I warned you what would happen, if one o' them girls got hurt.'

Kinney was getting wound up at the old men's power, maddened at their callousness, and his own helplessness. He'd watched the coach through his telescope, seen Jessica Dorne riding alongside Billy Mitten. From that moment, he thought of himself as some sort of archangel, that he alone had become responsible for her life – hers and Coral Kean's.

He stared dully at all the men seated around the

fire. 'What you got to ask yourselves is this,' he said. 'If those girls get harmed, the law will deal with you, and you'll be safe. But think what happens if the law don't get you . . . just think.'

'What you talkin' about, Sheriff?' The voice belonged to Munk Pawley, the deputy sheriff of Newburg.

'Jessica Dorne's got family in Eagle Spring. My guess is they'll hire a gun. Up there you can get someone mean enough to bite their gran'ma for a dollar – just for fun. Imagine what they'll do for a hundred . . . two hundred?'

'So you figure the United States government wants them murderers ridin' into Colorado, eh Sheriff? Cock-a-hoop with a big coach, a chest full o' gold an' their' killin ways?' Quirrel said with cynical contempt. There was chill in the old man's eyes and laughter rippled around the fire.

'I'm beginnin' to bore myself with this advice,' Kinney said. 'But it seems in some things, you men don't know your ass from holes in the ground. The safety of the innocent people – them girls – is my chief concern. That's what peace officers are elected to do,' he yelled desperately. 'An' God help us, that means protectin' the likes o' you! I'd rather all them that's accused get away, sooner than have the blood of them girls on my hands.'

'Accused?' Quirrel roared. 'The blood's on the hands o' Poole an' his depraved curs!' He surged forward suddenly, as if to rise.

Kinney held up his hand. 'That's twice you done

that Quirrel. Don't push me,' he said, and meant it. 'Yeah, the Chinaman's a killer all right, but not Poole. Not yet, not unless you force him. I talked to him in Eagle Spring. He'd have stood trial, if it hadn't been for you two despots. He didn't rate his chances, an' I kind of agree with him. But now you've got him cornered an' you don't know what he'll do, or even worse, that evil John China. From now on, any loss of life's down to you two.'

Quirrel rasped an obscenity, and Callister spat contemptuously into the fire.

'I know what your riders're gettin' for this,' Kinney said, the fervour in his voice holding all the men's attention as it resounded around the camp-fire. He glared at Quirrel. 'I also know what you pay your miners, an' what your gold poke could mean to 'em. For your kind, it really is the root of all evil.'

'Two thousand dollars for Poole's scalp. That's the latest offer,' Munk Pawley said.

Kinney turned to stare at him, aware of a sudden desolation, the violation of all things decent.

'Everyone else knows,' Pawley went on. 'No reason you shouldn't be left out, Sheriff.'

'Shut it, Munk,' Lane Manners said sharply.

'It's none of your goddamn business what me and Bewle's offerin',' Quirrel said. 'I got fifty thousand's worth of dust in that coach, so I got a right to offer any reward I want. And as for them wenches you keep harpin' on about, well let me tell *you*—'

'They ain't whores,' someone piped up.

Kinney looked up and saw young Lester Marden

118

sitting with his *compadre*, Darnley Finnis.

'Well, there's *one* of 'em ain't,' Marden said diffidently.

'An' you shut it too,' Callister told him.

'How the hell we know they ain't all together?' Quirrel demanded. 'Mitten, the women, Poole, eh? The four of 'em hell-bent on the Colorado line – how we know that? Women ain't exactly hog-tied are they?'

Kinney started to reply, but didn't, knowing his words were useless. He felt the oppression of Quirrel's bounty money. He knew about these tired, dirty cowboys in their scuffed boots and shabby working duds, their dollar a day and found, with chickory and beef meal. Instead of Jessica Dorne and Coral Keane, they'd be dreaming of treasure that night. Tomorrow, as the border loomed closer, they'd believe what Callister and Quirrel wanted them to. They'd obey orders, start shooting the horses that pulled the coach.

19

Making Out

Until after dark, working by lantern light, Will moved rock, shovelled dirt and gravel. The Chinaman held a gun on him and Poole came twice to watch his progress. Afterwards, when he studied what he'd done, he reckoned he'd have a fair chance of getting the coach up the hard-packed ramp. Given some sort of surface, the strongly-built Concord coach would get them to Colorado. Going back would be more difficult.

When he'd finished with his rock-piling, he saw someone had got a fire going not far from where he'd laid Charlie Chumser. He led the bays to the grass and water he'd seen seeping from the rock. It was a good spot to picket them for a well-earned rest before their final assault on the road. But as he got close, he suddenly hauled back on the lead's curb bit, startled and repelled.

Charlie Chumser was sitting by the fire. But it wasn't Chumser, it was Jessica Dorne. Chumser was on the ground wearing Jessica Dorne's clothes, complete with bonnet and shawl. He was stretched out on a coach blanket with some cloth wound tightly around his neck. Lovecraft's boots were back on his feet, and Coral Keane was kneeling beside him, applying face powder to his grey, lifeless face.

Jessica slowly turned her head, and looked up as Will approached. 'I had to,' she said. 'He told me it would likely save us all.'

'Well I guess that makes it all right, Ma'am?' Will said, uncertainly. He was still shaken by the spectacle, bizarre and ghostly in the firelight. He glanced over at Chumser, and saw they'd put white gloves on his hands. He gazed at Poole, long and thoughtful. 'Nice touch, but it won't fool 'em for long.'

'He's good enough for seein'. He ain't got to walk an' talk. They'll think they're seein' a dead girl . . . *not* Charlie.'

'Them goddamn Reavers know whose throat they slit. They was up *real* close, Frank. We're pretty sure they're workin' for Quirrel an' Callister.'

Poole looked over at Jessica, smiled grimly. 'You see, they never killed him . . . Charlie.'

'With his head hangin' off? Jeeesus, you goin' to try an' make 'em think *you* killed her?'

'Yeah. It's no more'n what I said I'd do. They'd be expectin' it. We'll just have to wait an' see,' Poole told him.

Will shook his head with incredulity as he led the

121

horses further away from the road. He was going to tie them into the trees where they'd be well concealed. The bank from which the timber road had been cut made an overhang. Anyone getting near, moving across the gravelly ledge on the slope above was sure to be heard. As would anyone on the road who got profiled against another big, early, moon.

While the Chinaman helped Will with the unhitching, Poole kept an eye on them. He walked in circles, his hand clutching and unclutching the butt of Will's Colt. Then, after they'd fed the horses, they ate skilleted hoe-cake and bacon. The Chinaman had his sitting up on the coach deck, keeping first watch.

Around the camp-fire. the four of them sat silent, absorbed in their own thoughts. The chill mountain held them in the clutch of its black, shadowy arms, as it did other men who schemed their downfall.

Will couldn't sleep, and at midnight when the Chinaman came off the coach to wake Poole, he gave up trying. His chains clinked faintly as he sat up and built himself a cigarette. As he smoked he heard a door of the coach scrape on a hinge, then saw Coral emerge and climb up on the deck. He fashioned a slow, wicked grin as she disappeared behind the feed-bags where Poole was taking his watch.

Then someone else moved and he saw it was Jessica. She was still wearing Chumser's coat, pants and blood-stained shirt. She also had on his hat, an old faded army cap that by some means played in the dark recesses of Will's memory. She sat near him, her

122

features nervous and tense in the pale, silvery-blue light.

Will laughed hollowly, and Jessica asked him what it was that touched him.

'Sorry, Ma'am, it must be somethin' to do with the moon. You got to be me to appreciate it.'

'I see,' she said, not fully understanding. 'I came to ask you, because you didn't say.'

'Didn't say what?'

'Should I have done this?' She tugged miserably at the lapel of Chumser's coat.

'It's up to you, Ma'am. Seems you gone an' done it anyway, so I'd say it was the right thing.'

'Thank you. Please call me Jess.'

They were silent for a time. Will smoked, Jessica jabbed distractedly at the embers with a switch. Then he said, 'Is there another dress you could put on? Somethin' white . . . undergarments even?'

'Why?'

'You can get out of here,' he whispered. 'Get back along the road. If you stay bank-side you could make it. This could be your chance to get away.'

Jessica shook her head slowly, holding his gaze. 'No,' she said.

He watched her for a long moment. 'Why didn't they chain the coach doors tonight?' he then asked.

'Coral knows I won't go anywhere.'

'Coral? You mean she won't either? Poole knows that?'

'He knows.'

'Why won't you go?'

'Too scared I guess. Perhaps I've just got used to her being around. Anyway, I've really nowhere to go.' She looked at him and smiled apprehensively. 'For me, Newburg was the start . . . an illusion. A Nirvana you might say.'

'*You* might say it, Ma'am . . . err, Jess. *That* sort o' talk's beyond my understandin'.'

Jessica smiled again. 'Newburg was only going to be the first stop. I want . . . wanted to go east. Oklahoma – St Louis even. But that was a few days ago, and things have changed. If I can help him . . . Poole, I will. I don't want him caught – not now.'

'You're feelin' the same as Coral?' Will asked her after a curiously hurtful pause.

'Good heavens no,' she said, 'but he's not a bad man – not like some would have us believe. I know it must be difficult for you, not allowing your one-time friendship to win you over. Then I doubt I'd admire *you* so much, if it was any different.'

Will coughed uneasily and embarrassed, flicked away the butt-end of his cigarette. 'Well, he can't go on outwittin' them,' he said. 'I know most o' the riders in that posse, how they think, reason things out. If it looks like we might make the border today, they'll start shootin' – call his bluff.'

'But he's going to make it look as if he *wasn't* bluffing,' Jessica said. She glanced over at the blanket that was covering Chumser.

Will shook his head doubtfully. 'I wish you'd go now, while you've got the chance,' he said. 'At least it'll be *one* of us safe.'

124

Then he saw the tears in her eyes and artlessly he reached out a hand. She took it, squeezed his fingers. 'Now you *really* know why I'm not going,' she said with a smile of relief.

'Yeah, guess I do,' he told her, looking at the bloodied shirt she was wearing. 'You ought to think about changin' them duds if we're gettin' down to sweet talkin'.

Up on the deck of the coach, nestling gently in the crook of Poole's arm, Coral stared into the interminable depth of the night sky. When she spoke her voice was slight and hushed. 'This is a good time for the tellin' I guess . . . so I will,' she said. 'I just want you to know that I wouldn't be too unhappy if we make it to Colorado. I just want you to know that.'

20

Draw from the Coulee

By the daybreak fire, Coral darkened Jessica's face and hands with dirt-water, and tucked her hair up under Chumser's plug hat. Then, after he'd made up the hitch, and with Coral's help, Will hauled the stubborn body of Chumser on to the coach deck. He laid the body face up, in full view of anyone watching from the rocky outcrops above. Jessica was inside near the window and, with Coral up on the box with Will, the coach set off.

The horses grunted and snorted uneasily as they began to haul the coach up over the slide, but Will had made a credible hard-packed dirt surface. As he steered the team cautiously on to the far side of the slide, the wheels dropped on their splinterbar. Then the coach veered in alternate directions as it lurched downhill, sliding forward against locked brake blocks. Aggressive eyes would be on them now, he thought. Men would be considering the body lying back on the deck, would catch a glimpse of Jessica Dorne posing as Charlie Chumser. As the sun rose they cleared the rockslide, made it through the steep-sided gully, and off on what would be the last leg of their southerly run. Below the road now, the rock and stunted pine fell sharply away, down to where the Pecos river started its long journey south to Texas and the Rio Grande. Ahead of them lay the Pecos badlands with its prickly pear and flame carpet of desert mariposa.

When the sun cleared the peaks of the Chimneys, Poole told Will to stop the coach. 'Give 'em enough time, they'll wonder why we stopped,' he said from the boot. He peered up at the slope above the coach. 'Plenty of cover there for 'em to creep up . . . have close look.'

Not fully understanding, Will tied in the reins, then built a cigarette. It gave him a weird, vulnerable feeling to be sitting there, knowing that men who knew him were more than likely watching. He wondered what his thoughts would be if he was them, what he'd do, how he'd react to the deception of Jessica Dorne's body.

'OK,' Poole said. 'Coral, you know what to do. Will, you and China have got to rid us of Charlie's body. He's goin' down to the Pecos . . . the quick route. I'm sorry, but there ain't no other way. Charlie was all right. He'd want to help us if he could – and he can.'

Will let Poole's reasoning sink in, stretched out to see the sliver of water that glistened far below. He knew no one would be climbing down there for a look at the body.

Poole poked the barrel of Will's Colt up through the boot opening. 'Will?' he asked. 'You listenin' to me?'

Will stood up, stepped back on to the deck where Coral was peering up the slope.

'China!' Poole called out. 'Go help the marshal. Somethin' to bring a smile back to that face o' yours.'

When the Chinaman didn't stir from the rear boot, Poole cursed. 'There'd be no goddamn trouble if the poor kid was alive,' they heard him say.

Coral glanced at Will. 'Come on,' she said quickly. 'I'll help you.'

Together they lifted Charlie's small body, moved it to the side rail of the coach.

'One swing an' out,' Will said wearily. 'Don't forget to let go.'

For a few seconds. like an immense white condor, Chumser seemed to fly. He took the breeze, winged out into the canyon. Then Jessica's dress folded, wrapped it's whiteness around the corpse. Chumser wheeled, then plummeted in his shrouded flight. But by then, Will and Coral had turned away.

Later, as the coach rolled further south, Will had the feeling he'd lost. He felt he might have done a lot more, had he taken advantage of opportunities when they'd come about. Poole, he knew, had counted on him putting the safety of Coral and Jessica first, ahead of his own personal and lawful interests. Poole knew he wouldn't escape, abandon the women. Up until now, he thought the posse would have urged caution, gone for close tracking and stakeouts. But now that posse had been fooled into thinking one of the girls had been murdered; killed in cold blood, as retribution for the rockslide. Maybe some of the men would be feeling guilty. Even the Reavers weren't natural women killers.

Will knew that Poole had bought himself another day of time, but that was all. When the horror of what they'd seen had worn off, there'd be no posse rider who'd feel benevolent or forgiving towards him. But then they'd figure it would only be a last resort for him to harm the second girl. Her death would mean the end of his bargaining ability – no reason for the posse to hold back. To Will's way of thinking, unless something stopped the coach in its final run north to the border, it would be that night or the following morning when the posse closed in on them.

Gradually the road left the canyon behind, and began its long, slow descent to the rim of the Pecos. There were fewer obstructions now, and they didn't stop to eat – just made good time. An hour before early dark they came to the crossing of the Las Vegas–Santa Fe stage route. That was where their new trail headed north to Arroyo Hondo, the border and Stonewall. Will briskly swung the coach and they raced on for several miles until Poole gave a new heading. He told Will to turn into a dry coulee that ran west into the brush. As they drove forward dust appeared, billowing low on the road behind them.

They came on to wagon tracks in the coulee, then they heard the distant but distinctive sound of a Sharps .50 rifle. When they came to a branching draw, Poole told Will to haul over and stop. Poole levered himself from the boot, stood peering ahead up the other draw. He saw more wagon tracks, but also those of cattle and horses. The air was heavy with the sickly reek of animal viscera and blood, and many buzzards wheeled lazily overhead.

'What's that gunfire?' Coral asked.

'Reavers. It's way out o' season, but by the stench, I'd say that's their skinnin' party,' Poole said. 'There's a wagon that'll have come up from Albuquerque. They freight the hides down to Mexico from there.' He shrugged, 'But it aint all bad news. Except them what's followin', we won't be runnin' into any law . . . not in these godforsaken parts.'

Will was worried though. He knew a skinning party was different, and wouldn't discriminate much between the hides of them and the cattle, particularly Coral and Jessica. It was more than likely they were the skinners who'd done for little Charlie Chumser.

They rode cautiously on, finally stopping at sunset to make camp.

'Don't unhitch 'em, Will,' Poole said. 'They can rest an' feed in their traces.'

The Chinaman took up his usual guard's stance atop a nearby boulder while the girls started a fire.

Will fed the horses, then watched Poole climbing the bank of the narrow draw.

With his badly bruised arm and shoulder, Poole awkwardly made his way up to a clump of barrel cactus. When he got there he dipped the brim of his hat and peered to the east. Then he looked west to where the sun had fallen into Arizona's Painted Desert. He stayed until it was nearly full dark, then came down for some of the Pass wine.

When the Chinaman had eaten what remained of the hoe-cake and bacon, Poole ordered him up to the cactus for his turn on watch. Ten minutes later, when he'd gained position, Poole moved closer to the fire, across from where Will was sitting.

'I've seen 'em,' he said. 'They lit 'emselves a big, early fire. Ain't too chary about bein' seen, that's for sure.' He looked into the darkening sky, at the small radiant smudge to the west.

But Will had already noted the distant fireglow. 'How'd you know it ain't them skinners?' he asked, although he knew himself it couldn't be. He simply wanted to establish the certainty of it being the Newburg posse.

Poole shook his head. 'Nah. They're to the east. It's the posse all right.' He moved his arm in a semi-circle. They must've rode through the brush . . . camp's about half a mile away.'

'What ruse you got in mind for tomorrow, Frank – 'cause you'll need one,' Will said, then turned to Coral and Jessica. 'You girls can't stay here with the coach. It aint the posse, it's them skinners . . . believe

131

me. Frank knows it too. At daybreak you're goin' to climb out o' the draw. You go up to where China's sittin' an' start walkin' towards that posse.'

In the evocative silence that followed, Will challenged Poole with his stare. 'In the mornin' they're goin' to break us apart. You can almost feel it,' he said fervently. 'There's nothin' you can do about it anymore. No more threats, no more o' nothin'. They'll be over us like. . . . We've known each other a long time, Frank.' He followed up with, 'You aint a bad man, but you'll probably be remembered for a lot o' bad *things.* Just don't let selfish an' cruel be two of 'em.'

Poole was quiet, thoughtful for a moment before he spoke again. 'If we're on telltale stuff, Will, perhaps now's the time to ask you somethin'.'

'What's that, Frank?'

'Way back when we was kids, you remember anyone mentionin' Quirrel or Callister?'

'Not when we was kids. Later on, yeah, o' course. Why?'

'Oh I dunno . . . been thinkin' on it for years. Old Rimmer came up from Utah with 'em. Peggy Mitten came too.'

'Yeah, reckon I know that, Frank. What you gettin' at?'

'I remember talk of an army bounty. Bought ranch land for Callister, minin' rights for Quirrel. Pa didn't get nothin'.'

'Well, *he* weren't army. He was a post trader, a sutler. Is there somethin' else you're thinkin'?'

'If they were army, they'd o' been from Fort Rawlins. That mean anythin' to you, Will? Fort Rawlins . . . Bitter Creek?'

'Yeah, you know it does. But like a lot o' things, that's somethin' long gone, Frank. Part of another time, another place.'

'Well it aint ever been "long gone" enough for me,' Poole rasped. 'Rimmer once told me about a Company from Rawlins got blue ticketed. He said he'd tell me one day, but he never did. That was one o' the reasons I came back . . . to find out.'

'Well whatever it was, Frank, I guess he died without lettin' on. Peggy . . . ma, never told me anythin' about it. An' now you reckon you've found the root of all them years of hurt. It's become your excuse for killing. An' I'm thinkin', Frank, that maybe Louis Callister an' Chester Quirrel didn't just die by happenstance. Maybe it was—'

'No,' Poole cut Will short. 'But maybe it's retribution, the weird sisters. Perhaps it's meant to be us . . . *me* that finishes 'em. Don't you need that much of a reason, Will?'

'No. I'm doin' my job. But perhaps now, I'm hopin' the end's goin' to be the same. Now, what about the mornin', Frank?'

Poole blinked hard. Then he smiled thinly, shook his head as he spoke. 'I won't be here in the mornin'. You won't be either, Will. We're takin' the coach.' He looked unhappily at Coral. 'But the girls stay.'

'Oh no,' Coral retorted. 'I aim to get where I'm goin' in that coach. I told you, remember?'

'That goes for me too,' Jessica said, looking at Will. 'I'm not afraid to stay. I think maybe I would be with that posse, though.'

'Believe me, you'd be afraid if you knew more about our predicament,' Will said directly. He looked over at Poole again. 'You goin' to move us out tonight?'

'Yep. I know this country, Will. The dark holds no fears. I'm trail broke from here to the border. By mornin' we'll be in sight o' Arroyo Hondo an' the Rio Grande.'

'Yeah, you hope,' Will said ruefully. 'You suppose they're goin' to just let us tippy-toe out o' here?'

'No, I don't, 'cause they'll have got the draw covered up ahead. That's where they'll be waitin',' Poole said. 'There's not one of 'em's thinkin' I'll turn back – not this far into our little jaunt. I know I'm plum played out, but they don't. They reckon I'm a bear with a sore head, an' feelin' real ornery.'

Poole had a moment's thought before continuing with his strategy. 'I know I only bought a day, but that's all I needed. We won't panic. We'll finish our supper real calm-like, then take measure. First off we'll muffle those bits o' clanky harness, then grease up the wheel bosses. We'll backtrack out o' here before the moon comes up.'

'They'll hear us, even if they aint watchin',' Will said.

'No they won't. They'll be jawbonin' around that big friendly fire o' theirs. We'll build our own – give 'em somethin' to see. After moonrise they'll be

134

watchin' an' listenin' – not before. Anyhow, Will, it'll be your job to move us out real quiet. You know the ground into the draw ... like Coral's face powder. We're goin' back the same way.'

'An' I'll be topsides,' Coral said unintentionally loud. 'I can shoot that carbine, if it comes to protectin' my honour.' She winked at Poole, and looked stubbornly at Will. 'Besides, that was a through ticket I bought in Eagle Spring.'

'And so was mine,' Jessica told them. 'I told the marshal how I feel. I haven't changed my mind.'

Frustrated, Will shook his head. 'That's different. Seems Coral's got herself branded with Frank's iron. I can't stop her.'

'No, and you can't stop *me either*,' Jessica said emphatically.

Will looked at her a moment, then without responding he got up. He went to the rear boot and got the grease pot, took the hubcap from the near-side front wheel and re-packed it. Then he slapped more grease around the pole swivel beneath the coach. The girls helped by, tearing cloth into muffle strips for the chains and bits.

When he crawled out from between the wheels, the girls had finished what they were doing, and Poole stood carefully watching him. Jessica was star-ing at him, the firelight dancing in her watery-bright eyes. He pulled her travelling bag from the coach, took it over to her and set it down.

'Take a dress out, put it over them goddamn boy's duds,' he said roughly. 'Come first light, you climb

that bank.' He pointed toward the side of the draw
where the Chinaman still lay beside the clump of
barrel cactus. 'I already told you ... walk west,
towards the posse. They'll see you before you see
them.'

'They won't be seeing me at all. I already told you,
Marshal, I'm not going.'

'Then you'll be stayin' right here. Goodbye Miss
Dorne,' he snapped testily.

'I'll follow on ... if I have to walk.'

'We're ready. Let's went,' Poole signalled
anxiously with a wave of the Colt.

For a moment Will hesitated, then with relief
showing in the slant of his shoulders, he picked up
the bag and placed it back in the coach.

21

Camp Clearing

Through his telescope, Morgan Kinney had seen the body on the deck of the coach as it rolled over the rockslide that morning. His thoughts and feelings on seeing the body shook him, drew out his contempt for the two men he held responsible. But it wasn't for much gain. They soaked up his anger with uncaring silence.

But some of the hard-bit members of the posse had been troubled by the sight of the body. When Will Mitten and Coral Keane were sighted dispatching the body into the canyon their feelings were even more stretched. But it was only Kinney that truly reflected on it, and decided it was something that would have to be paid dearly for.

When the initial shock of seeing it had eased, it dawned on the sheriff that the the spectacle of Jessica Dorne's body plummeting to the Pecos River had been staged for their benefit. Why hadn't Poole simply organized an alternative ending for the girl? At worst he could have left her body beside the road for them to find and take care of. There was undoubtedly something there that didn't add up, he thought. He knew enough about Frank Poole to know that whatever despairing straights the man was in, he was no cold-blooded girl-killer. Furthermore, Will would somehow have made himself an opening, created an edge. No way would he have had a hand in tossing Jessica Dorne's body over a cliff. There was something wrong and Kinney knew it.

As the day wore on and they trailed the coach north along the western side of the Chimneys towards Arroyo Hondo, he sensed the mood of the men was changing. He knew the shake-up of what had happened was wearing off. The faces he looked at were now just grim-set, the posse men feeling little responsibility or guilt for the girl's death. Those that did would simply foster new feelings of hatred for Poole. They wouldn't be listening to Kinney anymore, weary of watching and waiting. They wanted an encounter, and thirsted for blood and gold.

When they reached the Las Vegas – Santa Fe cross-roads and saw the dust-spoil of the coach heading north, the posse broke into a gallop. They knew their own dust would be seen from someone keeping look-out atop the coach, but their vitals were stirred. Kinney knew this was the beginning of the end, and unable to do anything about it, he kicked his spurs along with them.

When they came to the draw into which the coach had vanished, Bewle Callister saw the dust billowing low around the brush ahead of them, and hauled in his fine buckskin mare. He shouted, gesturing for the rest of the posse to go on with him.

The alkali dust was acrid, and choked their lungs, even through pulled-up neck scarfs. Sweat ran into the crimps of the riders' skin and salt stung their eyes. It was bad inside the coach too. Heat had condensed and the little wind fanned up by the run of the horses was stifling. Only when the dust from the coach ceased to billow did they rein in.

They heard the Sharps rifle fire, and Kinney guessed they were men from the main party of Reavers. He'd read and heard the reports of what was going on in and around the border States, and knew of the conflict between cattlemen and outlaws. With the extinction of the buffalo herds, ranch cattle were now being slaughtered for their hides. The guilty ones were riding from, and returning to hide out in the rough country north of the Pecos.

The coach moved on, and the posse followed until first dark when it stopped again. Callister led the posse back out of the draw, into the brush until they were less than a mile from the fugitive party's camp-fire. The men were wound-up but none of them wanted to advance on the coach along the draw, to ride into Frank Poole's desperate broadside of lead. They dismounted in a rocky clearing and Callister and Quirrel openly took command. Callister dispatched two men to hunt for rabbit or grounded chachalaca. Marley and Finnis were to take position in the draw, west of where the coach was stopped.

'We've got him now,' Quirrel said. 'Rat in a trap. We'll wait 'til the moon's up, then go in.'

'We'll split up,' Callister continued. 'We'll come at him from two sides . . . either end of the draw. Just remember, don't kill him 'less you got to. There's extra to the one that brings him in alive. He don't have to be standin', but that's three thousand if he's breathin'.'

'Four,' Quirrel rumbled. 'An' Bewle's right, he's no good dead. That heap o' money says I want to see his goddamn face . . . his eyes, when he suffers.'

'He'll be my prisoner,' Kinney suggested. But he knew his authority was bootless. God help Coral Keane and Will Mitten, he thought – he wouldn't be.

'Don't fret, Sheriff. You'll get your prisoner,' Callister snarled. 'He won't be lookin' his best, but you'll get him.'

They started up a big fire and fried off the remaining steaks. The weary, dust-encrusted men had smoked the last of their tobacco, and now, with the last of the beer and whiskey burning in their throats and bellies, they wanted to move in on their gold prospect, get back to Newburg and spend it. They lay on their blankets around the fire, waiting for moonrise. Some of them discussed how they'd rid themselves of four thousand dollars.

140

Callister and Quirrel's innate wickedness pervaded the camp. Kinney sat watching the pair of them, felt the force of their wealth and corruption. It was true that Franklin Poole had killed Louis Callister and, nearly ten years later, Chester Quirrel. It was a shocking twist of fate but, the presence of Poole now, his mere being alive, made a mockery of the old men's power. Studying them, Kinney realized that the slaking of vengeance was all they had left.

Quirrel was looking at Kinney. As if he'd just read his thoughts, he said. 'I'm uppin' that bounty to five thousand. Five thousand for him alive.' His voice was thick with whiskey.

'I've warned both o' you,' Kinney said. 'He's goin' to stand trial.'

'I'll match that,' Callister growled.

Quirrel looked around at the moody men. 'That sort of money'll buy you all you need ... keep you out of any law breakin',' he said, his voice heavy with implication.

It was for Kinney's benefit and he clenched his fists, shut his eyes tight. He thought that if there was anyone up there looking down, they too would probably be wanting to see Frank Poole safely across the border.

The moon was slow to rise over the Chimneys. It was as if it had had a look, and couldn't make up its mind whether to go back. But it quietened the men as its silvery-blue light washed over the men and their horses. Its rise also brought the dull sound of hoofbeats as Marden and Finnis who'd been posted as lookouts in the draw rode into the clearing.

The men dismounted and came straight to the fire, shook their heads about any doings to report. They took out their knives and hunkered down, speared at pieces of charred meat. Then Callister was on his feet giving details, naming the men who'd ride up the draw, those who'd ride back to keep watch. He'd be the one who'd lead the party that would attack from the far side of the draw. Valentine Quirrel would lead them that attacked from the near side. Their signal to attack would be one shot which he'd fire when everybody was in position and ready.

Kinney was waiting and when Callister had finished, he too got to his feet. 'Once again, Mr Callister's forgotten who's in charge o' this posse,' he said, the scorn in his voice seeking out Lane Manners. 'In fact as I'm the only worthy lawman here, you're all my representatives – much as it disgusts me.' The sheriff swung his gaze from Callister to Quirrel. 'Of course as long as we're up here I know I'm probably headin' for a bullet, or more likely headin' *away* from one. If that does happen, you're all seconded to Pick Hammond. That'll be his hard luck . . . avoidin' a bullet. But I doubt any o' you scum'll be prepared to go that far down the line.'

Kinney wondered what he'd do if he did ever get out of it, back to Newburg, whether he'd take off his sheriff's badge while he took care of Lane Manners and Munk Pawley.

142

'And in case any o' you are wonderin', he said, 'I don't believe it was Frank Poole killed that girl. I saw the blood – looked like someone more used to skinnin' beeves.'

When he paused, a different sort of murmur ran around the camp-fire. Callister looked as though he was about to crack apart with anger.

'Whatever happens, that girl's death will be investigated.' Kinney pushed on with, 'An' if somebody's bribed them Reavers, as God's my witness, they'll be decoratin' a cottonwood. Now finally, as long as you're goin' to attack the coach, you best listen to me. First off, nobody's ridin' down into the draw from this side. You'd have the moon at your backs, an' a bellyfull o' bullets. And nobody's goin' down into that draw to face up the coach. Against that alkali, a man'll make a good target, not that I could care a jack rabbit's jump. But I keep remindin' myself that Horse Creek Territory's payin' me to protect its citizens. So, we'll circle around, cross the draw where Marden an' Finnis were posted, and come down with the night sky at our backs.'

The men complied with Kinney's plan, and he got them formed on the far side of the draw. Above where the coach party's fire still sent up a thin column of smoke, he told the men to stay back while he rode forward. A few yards short of the rim, he reined in and dismounted, then crawled forward to a stony ridge.

'Poole . . . Frank Poole,' he shouted.

143

The name crossed the draw, bounced back around Kinney's head, up and down the scrubby alkali walls. Then the intense quiet prevailed again, and somewhere off to the west a grey wolf picked up it's lonesome howl.

'It's all over Poole. Before we come for you, send the girl out.'

Kinney's ultimatum sounded bizarre in the wild deserted country. He kneeled and listened to the disembodied echo of his own words, as those from the coach below would be.

After a full minute, he shouted again. 'Will? It's Morgan Kinney. Can you hear me?'

When there was no reply, no sound other than the uncanny echo, he slowly got to his feet. He drew his gun, moved forward to the very lip of the draw and looked down. Below him, cool moonlight bathed the emptiness of a camp-fire's embers.

'Well ain't that a goddamn shame,' anyone close by would have heard him mumble.

22

Under Fire

Through the starry, radiant night, the Concord rolled slowly, making little noise. For nearly a mile after leaving camp, Will walked the team back along the draw, then he climbed up to the driver's box. Poole settled himself behind the feedbags on the deck, and Coral was with him cradling the carbine. Jessica was inside the coach and the Chinaman was back in the rear boot.

When they came to the fork where they'd heard the gunfire of the skinning party, Poole indicated they make a sharp turn. The swollen moon spilled its waxy light into the draw behind them, making the alkali glisten like snow as they headed on to the north-west trail.

For two hours they travelled in overwhelming silence, pierced only now and then by a shrill snicker from one of the bays, or the distant howl of a timber

145

wolf. Then, when they rounded a long drawn-out bend, dark shapes suddenly scattered ahead of them. A cluster of wild brush steers that had been watering at a shallow tank fled, and scrambled up the shifting sides of the trail.

Because of the water, Will hauled in the team. He climbed down and pulled a bucket out from beside the chest in the front boot. He filled the bucket and offered it to the lead horse. After a moment, Poole climbed down. He watched Will for a moment then held the flat of his hand against the flanks of one of the team. Then he went behind the coach and did the same to Jale Stetter's horse.

'You think they'll make it?' he asked.

'I really don't know. Depends on all sorts o' things,' Will said.

'How about the Rio Grande . . . this side of Arroyo Hondo?'

'Yeah, maybe.'

Poole gazed up at the formation of stars that made up the Dipper. 'It's around midnight,' he said, forgetting that Will carried Huck Ambler's stemwinder. 'Without any hold-ups, I figure we'll be there by first light.'

Will shook his head. 'No we won't. This team aint runnin' flat out 'til sun-up.'

'Why not? They're bristlin'.'

'That's 'cause they're stage horses,' Will said. 'They know nothin' other than runnin'. They'll run 'emselves into the ground if you drive 'em to it.'

'How much rest they goin' to need?'

'One hour in every three or four. An' they'll need water.'

Worry carved itself across Poole's face. He shook his head slowly. 'That's an extra hour in the vicinity o' them . . . butchers.'

Will scooped up another bucket of tank water. He could have lied, said the horses would make it, let them run until their hearts burst. But it would have been the end for all of them, not just Frank Poole and the Chinaman taking the coach into Colorado. And he wouldn't want the women in a broken-down coach with the Reavers skinning party still around.

'Well, we'll just have to make up time when we're up an' runnin'. Let's go.' Poole said.

For the next hour the team pulled smooth and steady. Then the trail emptied into an arid wasteland. It was through this country that the coach would run in a series of undulating benches all the way to Arroyo Hondo. At the end of the second hour, Poole told Will to haul the coach into a broad fissure where cactus and mesquite screened them from the trail. Will stopped the team, and Poole pushed a bag of feed down from the deck.

Will was tiring of just about everything, and when he'd finished portioning out the feed oats, he threw the empty sack into the boot and grabbed a tin cup. With Poole watching closely, he poured a brimful of the Pass wine, and glared offensively at the Chinaman who was idly swinging the chain.

'You want some o' this drunk water?' he said, holding the cup out to Poole.

'I might, when you've got them chains back on,' Poole said with a dry smile. Then he motioned to the Chinaman.

'No, I meant it seriously, no tricks. For old times sake. You know, old friend to old friend. Might be the last time.'

'Yeah, an' skunks might smell sweet in the mornin'.'

The Chinaman chained Will to the off-rear wheel. He sat with his brandy, building a slim cigarette. As he flicked a match, the coach door opened and Jessica Dorne got out. She was pulling a blanket after her, and wrapped it around her shoulders as she sat near him.

Will smiled, sipped his brandy and smoked his cigarette. He wondered if any worry or fear had got to her yet.

'Where are we?' she asked.

'Not too sure. The horses'll let us know when we're near the river. That'll be Arroyo Hondo next stop.'

'We'll go on then . . . into Colorado?'

'There's nothin' to stop us.' He looked at her and smiled again. The tiredness and brandy worked on him and he closed his eyes for a moment. He didn't really believe there was nothing to stop them, just couldn't figure out what it could be.

Jessica was still there fifteen minutes later when he came to. Poole was calling his name.

'Sorry Will, but it's only rest-up time for the team,' he said.

They unchained Will and he breathed deep, stretching himself awake. He offered Jessica a hand up into the coach. 'Get yourself down real quick. Hug the floor if there's trouble,' he said with open concern.

They carefully walked the coach out of the rocky cleft back on to the trail. Now they moved due north through the dry, featureless landscape. There was the sweet scent of creosote bush in the air, and to the east, when Will saw the morning star, he knew they were heading for the day's first light.

With the first light of day, Poole had Will stop the coach again. Coral got down from the deck, and he told her to get into the coach and stay out of sight. He brought the Chinaman up on the deck to take her place, then they went on.

The sun was climbing, making its presence felt, when they first saw the skinning party. On a low, mesquite-covered rise, Poole spotted several hobbled horses. They were grazing beside a freight wagon, that was loaded high with cow hides. There was a small group of men standing around a camp-fire. Even from a distance it was plain to see they were rudely clothed, bearded and bedraggled, the unmistakable character of the Reavers and their skinning party.

Poole swore, and yelled for Will to pick up speed. 'Get the hell out o' here. Make this goddamn team run for its life – our lives.'

Deadmeat, a man of massive build, his face covered in a matt of tangled black hair, was the first to recover from the surprise of seeing the coach as it suddenly picked up speed. He swung up a big double-action army Colt he wore on a long lanyard around his neck. He fired at the coach, yelling an oath calculated to put fear into the driver and his passengers.

It did, and Will swerved the coach off the trail and into the cholla and wheel-high brush. He flicked out Huck Ambler's bull whip, cracked it around the lead team. The horses threw their heads in the air and broke into a wild headlong run. The coach lurched on its heavy thorough-braces and Will immediately swung it back on to the trail for more unhindered speed.

Poole spoke up. 'Won't take 'em long. Some o' their mounts looked ready-saddled. Can you keep them at a run, Will?'

'On this road for a while, yeah.'

'How long's that for chris'sakes, without 'em dyin' on us?'

'If we make the Rio Grande, I'll start believin' in the last round-up.'

23

Shortening The Odds

It was less than twenty minutes later when the skinning party came riding hard at the coach party from
across the brush. The coach team had caught the
tang of running water, and increased their eagerness
and speed. As they hit a long straight stretch, Poole
checked Will's Colt and handed it down through the
window to Coral, who levered a shell into the carbine.

'Here they come. It's goin' to be a turkey shoot
you won't want to miss, China,' he yelled derisively.

Will glanced to his left and slightly behind. There
were five riders racing through the brush. He saw the
barrels of their long guns come up, but it was the
Chinaman's Winchester that sounded first. The air
was split with the detonation, then again as a .50
Sharps rifle boomed across the barren land.

He felt, then almost in the same instant heard, the

crash as coachwood splintered below him, then a crushing pulse of air as another big bullet snarled past his head. He ducked low, jerked the reins hard, felt the run of sweat through his fingers. The firing increased in intensity between Poole, the Chinaman and the Reavers. Will swerved away from the trail again, offering up the rear of the coach and the deep boot as a reduced target. Then the Chinaman yelled and for a brief moment the gunfire ceased.

The riders veered to their right, trying to come in on the off-side of the coach again, but this time there was one less of them. The Chinaman's bullet had hit a horse high in the shoulder and its rider had fallen, hitting the ground hard. Now he was crawling through the alkali dust, desperately trying to make the safety of his stricken mount.

'They're tryin' to get between us an' the trail.' But as Poole shouted, the trail suddenly dipped, and the brush thinned. Ahead and below them was the Rio Grande. Its level was rising, but not yet swollen and deep from distant Rocky Mountain melt water.

The trail bent west, and followed the course of the river towards the Arroyo Hondo crossing point. Will swung the team hard. The firing started again as the Reavers saw the coach making for the ford. Above the brush and against the light, Will saw the bodies of the riders, their rifles and the horses' heads as they closed in fast, crying spine-chilling oaths.

Through the side window of the coach, Coral saw the nearest rider swing his spotted pony alongside. He carried his rifle in the crook of his arm, and grinned broadly with a mouthful of decayed teeth as he pulled the trigger at point-blank range. The gun shot blasted into the coach, its echo torturing her ears and the bitter smell of powder rasping her eyes and throat. The Chinaman's boots madly scraped the deck as bullets from the .50 calibre rifles tore into the white-oak panelling. Another rider came alongside the coach and made a target that couldn't be missed. Coral raised Will's Colt and fired a single shot. The man yelped, and coughed blood. He rolled forward on to his horse's neck, futilely grabbed its mane before rolling to the ground. The axles barked and cracked as the wheels recoiled from a backbone of small boulders. The whole superstructure of the coach bounced high in its leather braces, then crashed heavily to the ground again as they raced on.

Will heard a sickening thud from behind him, then felt the Chinaman's body hit him between the shoulders. With his left hand he reached around him and dragged the body half into the driver's box. The Chinaman's gimlet eyes stared up at him with no regret or remorse. His head twisted, and the black, shiny pigtail brushed against Will's leg. Then the dying man spat vilely and Will heeled him out between the breeches of the racing team. He watched, as for a moment, the body caught the horses' flashing cannon bones before disappearing beneath the coach.

'So long, feller. Whoever he is, give your god a hard time when you meet,' he said without feeling.

At that moment there was another volley of fire and the near horse of the lead team broke stride, stumbled and went down. The coach rammed into the wheel horses with such force that Will was almost thrown from the driver's box. As the horses whinnied, snorted their terror, Poole thrust the Winchester into Will's hands.

'Get down bankside,' Poole shouted as he scrambled over the deck rail.

Without aiming, Will wing-shot a moving figure in the brush, then swung himself to the ground. Poole flung the coach door wide and Coral almost fell out with Will's Colt still in her hand. Jessica followed, her eyes cloudy, her face drawn with worry.

'You'll be OK, there's cover here. They're down to three – we'll hold 'em off 'til the posse gets here,' Will yelled, with almost discernible hope in his voice.

There was a stunt pine that rose up from a cleft in some moss-covered boulders and it twisted to the water below. Coral handed Will cartridges and with some relief, he pressed them into the breech of the Winchester. Coral took the carbine from Poole, and handed him back the Colt while she reloaded from a cartridge belt. Then she took a position with her feet at the water's edge. She gripped the rifle, steadied it firmly against the bark of the gnarled pine.

'Yeah, we'll hold 'em off. I'm only worried who'll come at us from the other side o' this river,' she said drily.

The horses were unnerved but didn't want to move. They sagged miserably in their traces, their sensitive ears hurting from the noise of the guns. But now only the roil of the watercourse made a sound. Black vultures spiralled high, making great swooping circles above where the skinners had spilled their blood across the brush.

Suddenly harsh, piercing yells erupted from the brush again and gunshots ripped the silence apart. From the west, north and south, the three remaining skinners closed in on the coach. They got close, their big bullets chipping and whining against the rocky bankside as they rode forward at speed.

The big, black-haired rider came charging through the brush. He was broadside to the coach, and it was him that Will calmly drew a sight on. He let out his breath and squeezed the trigger of the Winchester. There was no movement from the man on the heavy-built dun; he still held his army Colt out ahead of him. It was only when he placed a long hunting-knife across his mouth, clenched it between his teeth, did Will know he'd hit him. Will had aimed for the man's broad, wolf-skin covered chest and, knowing he hadn't missed, took a sharp look to his left and right.

Poole was standing knee-high in the water, the carbine in his right hand. The skinner who rode in from the south was almost on top of him, leaping from his horse beside the stunt pine. Will immediately looked back to the rider he'd shot, saw him crash into the off-side wheel of the coach, his great head breaking spokes as he impaled himself across the boss of the axle.

From where he'd stood resolutely shielding the girls, Poole was falling backwards into the river. He'd been hit bodily by the skinner who'd already taken a bullet from Coral's Colt. But the man was tough, and was seeking to drive his knife sideways into Poole's neck. Coral screamed and Jessica took the gun from her. Using both thumbs, she drew back the action and fired point-blank into the middle of the man's greasy, tight-jacketed back.

Will swore, turning to see the third rider swerving his horse away. 'You take this message back to any scum that ever figures on riding into Horse Creek Territory,' he said. With that he calmly pumped three bullets into the fleeing skinner. The man fell forward, then toppled backwards before rolling from the saddle. His trailing boot caught in the stirrup and he screamed as he thrashed through the thorn and prickly scrub. 'Some o' that punishment'll be from Charlie Chumser an' some from me,' he rasped. 'An' probably from a lot of other kind an' peaceable livin' folk,' he added quietly.

He looked back to the river and saw Poole with one foot on the bank. He was holding on to the carbine, and had it pointed at Will's middle.

'What you thinkin', Will?' he asked.

'Oh, all sorts o' things. There was somethin' I remember Peggy Mitten sayin'. I think it was about corn seed.'

'What you mean "corn seed"? Poole asked, wiping the water from his eyes.

'She said to plant 'em in fives. I guess she really meant "skinners".'

Poole laughed. 'Yeah, maybe she did. But what else you got on your mind, Will? Why you pointin' that goddamn carbine into my soakin' bread wallet?'

'Because now you're my prisoner again.'

24

Last Move

From somewhere across the Rio Grande a distressed quail made its shrill comment and, beneath the roots of the stunt pine, a nest of provoked water moccasins writhed in lethal circles. Then for another long moment, before Poole spoke, the desert claimed its usual crushing silence.

'It's mighty peaceful now, but you might as well pull that trigger, Will,' he said.

'Yeah, I been thinkin' on that Frank. In truth you ain't my prisoner, 'cause this ain't Horse Creek Territory. But then I ain't ever been too strict on fences or borders.'

Out of the corner of his eye, Will saw one of the water snakes swimming towards the foot Poole still had in the water. He jerked his rifle, shouted for Poole to move. But in that instant Coral threw herself at him. Poole saw the advantage and rushed forward, swinging his clasped fists into Will's face. He grabbed the rifle, turned and smashed the stock wildly at the long venomous snake. Then he backed off and dragged at the collar of Will's jacket.

The marshal was only out for a second, and then Poole heard him mumbling, 'I wasn't goin' . . . you aint wanted. . . .'

But when he fell, Will hit the back of his his head on the stony bank, and he went back into a dark, thoughtless limbo.

It was five minutes later that he opened his eyes, and a single thought process started to work. Jessica was watching him, with the Winchester pointed up into the big blue sky.

He sat up, wincing with the hurt across his eyes. Then he snatched at the rifle and wondered about Jessica not saying a word or trying to stop him. He looked across the river, saw Coral astride Jale Stetter's horse. Frank Poole was beside her, waist high in the current with a hand clasped to the saddle horn. Will squinted, watching them as they made the far bank. Without looking back, Poole took Will's Colt from Coral and pushed it into the waistband of his pants.

'What do you think he left this for?' he asked, broodingly levering a shell into the Winchester.

'He didn't say. Maybe he wanted to leave you with the choice. Shoot him or let him go.'

Will sighted up, breathed shallow as his old friend started walking towards Arroyo Hondo, then presumably the Colorado border.

'Bang!' he said, and carefully laid the gun at his feet.

'I knew you wouldn't – so did he,' Jessica said.

He looked tired and kindly at her. 'Look,' he said. 'First I got no jurisdiction this far west. Second, my hands are shakin' too much for a clean shot. Third, anythin' that hurts Quirrel an' Callister's got to be for the good. An' fourth, there ain't ever been proof of him doin' any illegal killin'. In fact he's done us all a favour. Can you imagine four o' them power-crazed megalomaniacs? I guess *that's* why I never pulled the trigger.'

'I know, Will,' she told him supportively. 'I did learn something of the man in the last few days. Now it looks like he's chosen Coral Keane over fifty thousand dollars.'

Will leaned back and took out the last of his tobacco. Slowly and carefully he built a cigarette, then lit it with one his few remaining matches. 'There was somethin' he was goin' to tell me about Quirrel an' Callister. Somethin' that happened a long, long time ago. Now I guess I'll never know.'

'What will you do now?' she asked, after he'd taken his first long draw.

'Wait for the posse. Wait to see the looks on some o' them mean faces. Work out how to re-rig the team . . . get us back to civilization.'

'I meant after – back in Newburg.'

Will smiled. 'Think about how I'm goin' to fill in the paperwork. Sort out one or two things with Lane Manners. I reckon there's no place left for my sort o' marshalin' – not as long as the likes o' Quirrel an' Callister are around.'

'There's got to be something in your favour.'

'Yeah, one thing. If they bump into that skinner, an' his mouth's still workin', maybe he'll tell 'em about my sort o' punishment.'

'There's no other way you can keep your job . . . in a more peaceful line?'

'Hah,' Will said. 'Maybe there is at that. I'll tell 'em Frank Poole might come back.'

Jessica smiled back at him. 'And if that doesn't work?'

'I hear they're givin' away range land in Kansas. I'll take me a wife an' go there.'

'You'll take a wife?'

'Yeah. If you've a mind, that is. I got some money saved . . . could build us a house.'

'What sort of house?'

'Any sort, Ma'am. As long as it's bigger than that goddamn coach . . . if you'll excuse my turn o' speech.'